CHERRINGHAM

A COSY MYSTERY SERIES

LAST TRAIN TO LONDON

Neil Richards • Matthew Costello

]

RED DOG
UK

Published by RED DOG PRESS 2020

Originally published as an eBook edition by Bastei Lübbe AG, Cologne, Germany, 2014.

ISBN 978-1-913331-62-7

www.reddogpress.co.uk

Cherringham is a long-running mystery series set in the Cotswolds. The stories are self-contained, though many will enjoy reading them in order of publication:

1.

A BUMP IN THE NIGHT

OTTO BRENDL WOKE with a start.

He'd been dreaming, dreaming of home far away and a long time ago. But now he was wide awake, his head instinctively raised just inches from the pillow so that he could hear better, his eyes staring into the pitch darkness, trying to make out the shapes of his familiar bedroom.

He was sweating.

From fear? he asked himself.

No.

It's July – even here in England it gets hot in July.

But he knew it wasn't the summer heat that had woken him. He'd heard a noise downstairs. A creak on the floorboard in the kitchen. His little burglar alarm, that loose floorboard – he had never fixed it.

A good thing too. Living alone all these years, always afraid of a break-in, even though he never kept any of his stock in the house.

Slowly he swung his legs out from under the duvet and onto the carpet.

Reaching for his walking stick, he leaned firmly on it and stood up, his knees creaking. Now that his eyes were getting used to the darkness he could make out the familiar shape of the dressing table and the half-open door.

He picked up his house keys from the dressing table. Then he went through the doorway, bare feet padding silently on the carpet, and stood still on the landing, moving his head slowly from side to side trying to hear more. He held his breath and concentrated on the sounds of the house, listening out for anything unusual.

No sound. As if from nowhere a cool trickle of air caught the side of his neck: a draught. There was no doubt about it. A window had been opened. Or a door.

Downstairs.

So someone had tried to get into the house. Or maybe… *they were still in the house.*

If it were burglars they would be disappointed. They would find no silver, no gold – although he was a jeweller by profession. He was old, but he wasn't a fool: he kept no valuables in the little cottage – no conventional valuables anyway. Certainly nothing the average thief would be attracted to.

But there were things that a burglar might take almost by accident, not realising the value they held – for Otto. Objects that had – what did they call it? – *sentimental* value. A burglar might take them, throw them in a bag, and tomorrow swap them for a few pounds in some backstreet junk shop. Leaving him weeping at their loss.

He headed for the stairs, suddenly determined that whoever was down there was not going to get away with it. He felt a rush of anger.

"Who's there?" he shouted, his voice filling the stillness. "I've called the police, they're on their way."

His hand firmly clasped on the smooth banister, he took the stairs as fast as he could, tapping the stick on each step in the darkness.

"I know you're down there," he called again as he reached the wooden floor of the hallway.

His hand fumbled for the light switch – he flicked it on, almost flinching at the brightness, half expecting a man to be there, readying himself for some violent attack.

But the hallway was empty. He listened again. He could still feel the draught, but there was no sound.

He walked silently into the kitchen and turned on the light. The back door was just ajar.

Someone had definitely been in.

Perhaps they were still in the house?

Otto knew he had locked up before he went to bed. He had done every single night of the twenty-four years he had lived in Cherringham: as regular as clockwork — *well, I'm a jeweller, what do you expect?*

But someone — someone very clever, for these were good locks — had slipped into the house while he was asleep. Why? He must check on the *children*.

He gently closed the back door, then turned and headed back down the hallway.

"If you are in the house," he called out again, "There is still time to make your escape before the police come and we will say no more of it."

He said all this as much to strengthen his own spirits as to scare away the intruder.

At the end of the hallway was the sitting room. He switched on the light and scanned the room. Spotless, as usual. Nothing taken — not even the jar of pound coins he kept for the parking machine in the village. He turned and approached the most important room in the house — the little box room.

He tried the door handle. It was locked: a good sign.

Holding his ring of house keys in one hand, he carefully went through them until he found the right key. He inserted the key in the lock and opened the door.

He flicked the light switch, still prepared for the worst.

And then breathed a deep sigh of relief.

There on the shelves, in their velvet-lined cases, were his puppets, their glass eyes staring sightlessly back at him, their bright colours vivid in the electric light. His Kasperle, his Petrouchka, his wonderful Kersa King and Queen.

His children were safe.

Whoever had broken into his little cottage had not been interested in the puppets. His precious collection, gathered in markets and auctions across Europe over the years, was probably now worth thousands of pounds – but only an expert would know that. No, whoever had broken in had surely come looking for gold and had gone away disappointed.

He scanned the rest of the room. Everything was neat and tidy, just as he always left it: the workbench, the rolls of fabric, the tools, the half-made puppets – the little theatre in panels, all ready for tomorrow. All safe.

But the big old wicker basket on the floor was at an angle.

Had he left it like that? Surely not. He knelt down and slowly raised the lid, suddenly anxious. But no, there was no need to worry. Nestled together in the folds of bright striped curtain fabric lay his old friends, just as they should be.

"My beauties," he said, reaching in his hands to touch the puppets.

There was Punch, red-faced, grinning, his big nose outrageous. And Judy – long-suffering, old for her years. Next to them the Policeman, mouth ever-open in outrage. The green Crocodile, teeth bared. The sausages. The truncheon. The Baby. The Hangman.

And the Devil, with fangs, fork and horns – guaranteed to bring a squeal of fear from the little ones, sitting on their mothers' laps.

"I know, I know – it's night-time," he said, closing the lid. "And we have a busy day ahead. But I wanted to be sure you were all safe and sound."

He got up, turned the light off, and shut the door, locking it with the key. Then, with one last tour of the cottage to make sure there truly was no one hiding in the shadows, Otto turned the lights off and went back upstairs to bed.

He must try to get some sleep for he had to be up early.

But he still felt uneasy. Someone *had* been in the house and, he wondered, how had they got through those locks? What were they looking for? And why did they take nothing at all? Not even the little jar of coins. It was puzzling, and Otto Brendl did not like puzzles.

Not then, not now.

Still, all was secure – and there were hours before dawn and the big day ahead.

OUTSIDE, IN THE sweet-scented garden, the man waited until the bedroom light went off and then, taking care to stay in the shadows, moved quietly across the lawn away from the house.

In the soft light of the moon, he could see his footsteps in the wet grass – dark tell-tale patches.

But that is not a problem. They will melt away long before the old man wakes, he thought.

All had gone well. There had been no dog. He had managed to avoid the security lights. The locks had obeyed the tools that he carried with him. The old man had not woken until after the job had been done. And he had executed the task to the best of his ability.

Executed. *Yes…*

Now he must wait until the fuss blew over – for there would be a fuss, of that he was certain.

Then he would tidy up, and go home with no one the wiser. And then, finally, this long journey would be over.

He turned his back on the house, climbed the wire fence and

made his way along the side of the ploughed field, up the hill towards a small copse.

The night was so quiet.

At the copse, he dragged his old sports bag from under a pile of leaves, took out the sleeping bag inside and made himself comfortable. He would sleep until dawn. Nobody would see him here. But from where he lay, he could see right across the valley.

Down below, the old man's cottage was quiet. Beyond it, further down the hill, spread a valley of fields, misty in the moonlight. He could just make out the silver ribbon of the Thames meandering across the fields, a little line of boats moored upon it.

And to one side the village – small town, really – of Cherringham, fast asleep. He pulled his sleeping bag up to his neck – and then he slept too.

2.

ALL THE FUN OF THE FAIR

"OKAY. WHAT'S THE point of winning coconuts anyway?" asked Jack. "Aside from making piña coladas, that is."

Sarah pointed to the corner of the coconut-shy and Jack dutifully stacked his box of coconuts on top of the others.

"It's a tradition, Jack," she said. "Like your turkeys at Thanksgiving, Easter Parade. It's what we do here."

Jack tilted his head, looking entirely sceptical.

"Well, I'll believe it when I see it."

"Trust me," said Sarah. "Now, Daniel – grab the hoops and show Jack how to set them up, would you?"

She watched as her son – now a two-year veteran of the Cherringham Primary School Summer Fête – headed off with Jack to the car to get the heavy iron hoops and the mallet.

Hectic as it always was, the fête was still one of the high points of Sarah's year, when the village put on its best face and she felt genuinely happy to be out of London and back into country life.

For some reason that she couldn't quite remember, she'd been handed the coconut-shy to organise a couple of years ago, and it had just been assumed then that she'd always manage it.

More tradition in action, she realised.

Her daughter Chloe had come along last year to help – but this year she had reached the age where a primary school fête had become seriously uncool. Sarah, on the other hand, loved the whole day. The smell of the freshly cut grass, the bustle of parents and teachers racing the clock to get the fête ready, the excitement of kids free at last from the school year with the summer holidays stretching ahead of them.

"I thought we'd push for two pounds a go this year, Sarah, what do you think?" came a voice from behind her which she instantly recognised. "We so desperately need the money!"

Sarah turned. Mrs Harper, the headmistress, stood frowning, uncertain. Loved by all the kids, but hopelessly disorganised, Mrs Harper was a throwback to a time in education when management skills came second to passion.

"Or is it too much? Yes, it's probably too much. A pound? Or perhaps one pound fifty? What do you think?" she said.

"Why don't we charge a pound," said Sarah, smiling. "But offer three for the price of two?"

"Brilliant!" said Mrs Harper. "Like at the supermarket – buy one get one free. Bogof – isn't that what they say? Or should that be b-t-gof? Hmm. Anyway, must crack on – there's a row brewing on the white elephant stall and I'm told they need a peacemaker."

And off she strode towards the line of little white stalls which lined the playing field.

With an hour to go before the fête opened, Sarah could see it was all coming together. The dog-show arena was up – and the PA caravan already pumping out music. The ice-cream van was open. The merry-go-round for the little ones had started spinning, and the bouncy castle was fully inflated and ready for action; a splash of orange against the bright blue summer sky.

On the patch just opposite the coconut-shy, Sarah could see the local fire engine all set for a display and – talk of tradition! – old Mr Brendl was putting the final touches to his Punch and Judy stall. In fact – she suddenly realised – the only stall which didn't look ready was her own.

Where were her workers?

On cue, Daniel and Jack appeared from around the back of the stall, finishing what looked like two very large ice-creams. Jack grinned sheepishly at her.

"Daniel here was just introducing me to the 99," he said. "An ice-cream with a stick of chocolate in it. This would *kill* back in the States. You Brits sure know how to live."

"We know how to work too," she said. "Now pick up that mallet, soldier, and get hammering."

JACK TUGGED ANOTHER piece of pink cotton candy from his stick and popped it in his mouth. 'Candy floss' they called it here – which was kinda ironic since you'd definitely need to floss your teeth after eating it.

As soon as he'd finished setting up the coconut stand – the 'shy' they said – Sarah had suggested that he go explore the fête, check out all the offerings. And as someone who had taken his own daughter to so many tacky church carnivals, a lot was similar.

But then – a lot wasn't.

White Elephants, Pin the Tail on the Donkey, sure. But then – 'Welly Wanging'? Really? And something called 'Tombola' – kind of a raffle. There were things going on here he could hardly describe, let alone understand.

"Mr Brennan!"

Jack turned, to see Tony Standish at one of the little stalls.

"Hey, hello, Tony," said Jack. "They got you roped in too, huh?"

"Wouldn't miss it for the world, old boy," said Tony.

Jack had come to consider Tony – a Cherringham solicitor and an old friend of Sarah's family – a friend as well.

"Care for a 'lucky dip'?" he said, gesturing to a large container filled with slips of paper. "Three tickets for a pound. If your number ends with a nought or a five, it gets you one of these fantastic prizes!"

Jack inspected the table, filled with candies, bottles of wine, chocolates, mysterious packets of English cakes and the grand prize: a quart of whisky.

Raffles and prizes – now *that* Jack could understand.

"Sure," he said. "I'm feeling lucky today."

He handed over his pound, reached in and pulled out three tickets. Tony took them and opened them up one at a time.

"No… no…" said Tony, dramatically opening up each ticket. "Yes! We have a winner, ladies and gentleman! Lucky number 405!"

Tony had missed his calling. He would have made a great barker!

Jack checked the table. Was it the whisky? The wine?

Tony handed him a small packet of chocolate biscuits.

"Wagon wheels!" Tony said. "How perfectly appropriate!"

"You don't say," said Jack, looking at the wagon train image on the front of the pack. "Guess pardner, it's time I hit the trail."

He put the packet in his pocket, said his thanks to Tony and headed back towards the coconut-shy.

At first, it seemed that Sarah had quite a crowd ready to play – but in fact most people were watching a ladder display by the Cherringham firemen. And over by the Punch and Judy stall, a sea of kids were already sitting with their mums and dads on the ground, impatiently waiting for the first performance of the day. Seemed like it was showtime but the show hadn't begun.

In fact, the coconut-shy had no customers at all. Sarah stood by the boxes of coconuts while Daniel was half-heartedly throwing balls at the hoops.

"Just in time," said Sarah. "We need things shaking up a bit here, Jack – we've only taken about ten pounds so far."

"You ever thought that maybe you should give out prizes, not coconuts?" said Jack.

"Don't be silly, *everybody* loves coconuts. They just need to know how easy it is to win."

"And Mum says you're going to show them," said Daniel.

"Oh, really?" said Jack.

"Absolutely," said Sarah. "You're going to bring some all-American chutzpah to the whole thing. World Series atmosphere. Razzamatazz. Hullabaloo."

She handed him five of the heavy wooden balls.

"It's just like baseball. But without the helmets."

"What if I don't play baseball?"

"Don't be ridiculous. I've seen the films. *All* Americans play baseball."

Jack looked at the metal hoops and the coconuts stuck in each one.

"That's a pound by the way, Jack."

"And this – is coercion."

"I prefer to call it donating to a good cause," said Sarah with a grin.

"You're going to owe me for this," he said, shaking his head.

But Jack knew he had no choice. He walked over to the little paint mark on the grass and inspected the wooden balls.

When was the last time he'd pitched a ball?

His mind ran back to the local Little League field back in Bay Ridge. He and Katherine used to help out with the coaching when their daughter played. Sometimes it seemed like the games were more for the parents than the kids.

They certainly brought everyone together.

The memory – now, here – suddenly alive, suddenly too close. Imagining his wife on those sunny golden days before she got ill…

Time to throw the ball, he thought.

Without a warm-up, this could hurt.

"Go Jack!"

From nowhere Daniel had gathered a bunch of his pals to watch – they cheered, jumping up and down. And Sarah mysteriously had conjured up some of her village friends who began clapping.

Jack had a sneaky feeling he'd been set up – but there was no escape. He had to throw and make it good. Anything else would be un-American!

He looked at the targets and picked the coconut that looked most likely to pop out of its hoop. Then, playing to the crowd, he went into his old pitching routine – funny how it came back after all these years – staring at the ground, rocking gently on his heels, winding up the energy, then bringing his arm back, ready to release and —

A scream from behind him cut through all the noise of the fête.

Harsh, full of fear, of horror – instantly recognisable as real.

This wasn't someone playing about.

3.

THE PUPPETEER

JACK TURNED AND dropped the ball.

Across the grass at the Punch and Judy stall, parents stumbled to their feet, grabbing children, hurrying away. The screams kept filling the air – made more horrifying on such a beautiful summer's day.

His eyes focused on the Punch and Judy stall, its red-and-white striped curtains still tightly drawn.

A woman stood to the side of the little stand-up theatre, arms limp. Her face blank with shock; eyes wide, mouth open, breathing fast.

Her eyes locked on what lay at her feet.

And Jack now knew why she had been screaming.

The head and shoulders of a man were visible, sprawling out from the stall, motionless, eyes wide open. As soon as Jack saw him he knew it meant only one thing.

Immediately his old training kicked in. When other people ran away, Jack ran *towards*…

Behind him he heard Sarah telling Daniel to stay back. Then as he pushed through the retreating crowd and approached the stall, he felt her come level with him, reaching out for the woman.

As Sarah drew the woman gently back, he knelt down by the man on the ground, the Punch and Judy puppeteer wearing a satiny costume of red and blue.

His right hand was inside the puppet Punch, ready for the show – its cheeks painted rosy, eyes glinting and a broad grin carved into the plaster of its face stretching from ear to ear.

Jack moved fast. The man wasn't breathing. There was no pulse.

Jack's hands went to his chest and he began pressing.

The puppeteer's eyes remained glassy and unresponsive. His thin wispy white hair rustled as Jack pressed rhythmically on his chest. The man's glasses lay beside him, crushed by the fall. His eyes remained wide open.

Then – a detail, even as Jack kept up his rhythm.

The man's teeth were clenched tight, as if he'd been in extreme pain – and on his lips were flecks of foam.

"Heart attack?" said Sarah, now kneeling next to him. "Someone's gone for a defibrillator."

Jack looked up, ready to say… *might be too late for that.* Instead, noticing her face, he said:

"Could be, don't know how long he hasn't been breathing."

Jack quickly removed the puppet from the man's hand then straightened his body. He tilted the man's head back making sure that the airway was clear and then clamped his fingers tight onto the old man's nose and started mouth to mouth.

He counted the breaths, then pulled back so Sarah could continue the CPR, applying pressure to the chest.

He looked up — a small crowd had formed around them.

"Need an ambulance, fast," he said firmly. "This isn't doing… and where is the…?"

Jack had been with people – some in the line of duty – who had slipped away before his eyes. That moment always seemed like the one thing he couldn't accept.

A moment when he could do nothing.

Then one of the firemen hurriedly squatted next to Jack and

Sarah and folded open a portable defibrillator. Jack paused his mouth to mouth.

"Shirt?" he said to the fireman, who nodded as he pulled the cables from the defibrillator box. If there was the slightest chance at all, they had only seconds.

Sarah drew back as Jack pulled open the man's collar, and then ripped open the shirt, tearing the fabric back. The fireman passed the sticky pads to him, and Jack pressed one high on the man's chest, the other lower down on the other side.

As the machine began to build a charge, Jack took a second to examine the man who lay before him.

"Do you know him?" he asked Sarah.

"It's Mr Brendl," said Sarah. "Everybody knows Mr Brendl."

"Stay back," said the fireman.

The machine delivered its jolt of electricity.

"Ambulance on its way," said someone.

Then the fireman reached in and continued mouth to mouth, while Jack took over pumping Mr Brendl's chest.

The minutes went by, with the fête now silent, the music stopped, the rides motionless, as if everyone was willing the old man to live.

Jack felt a hand on his shoulder – the ambulance had arrived. The fireman nodded to him to remove the defibrillator pads. He peeled them off.

And then he spotted another detail, in the hyper-reality of that moment. Underneath Mr Brendl's armpit was a small tattoo. A faded blue tattoo of a bird.

But not a pretty bird. Not a bird of peace. Not a robin, or a dove. No.

A vulture.

And that stopped Jack.

Thinking: *I've seen that before. But where?*

And then, he pictured it. Back in the nineties when the Russian mobs had moved in on Brighton Beach, Brooklyn, he had seen this tattoo on the body of a bloated fat cat whose days of Stoli and caviar had ended with him washed up on the rocks of the Brighton Beach jetty.

And now – the same tattoo, here.

In Cherringham.

The paramedics lifted Brendl onto a stretcher and moved him quickly to the ambulance. Jack and Sarah stood up and watched them go.

"Do you think – there's a chance? That he might —?" said Sarah.

Jack hesitated, which he guessed would be answer enough. Then: "They'll do what they can," he said. "And we – we did what we could."

But while Jack hated the fact they hadn't saved the old man, something else bothered him now.

Brendl… Brighton Beach. Was there a connection?

Jack told himself to go easy.

It's a heart attack. Takes people every day. End of story.

That's what he told himself.

But that tattoo. The vulture.

Is there something wrong here? he thought.

4.

BACK TO SCHOOL

"KINDA FEEL WE'VE done something bad," said Jack, folding his arms and squirming on the too small chair.

Sitting next to him in the tiny reception area of Cherringham Primary School, Sarah thought he looked like an over-sized schoolboy. And a guilty one at that.

The reception – four small chairs and a coffee table – was guarded by the school secretary who sat in her office behind a glass wall. Sarah smiled at her. The secretary peered back over large glasses and went back to her work.

When Sarah got the call from Mrs Harper, the head teacher had still sounded rocked by Mr Brendl's now-confirmed heart attack.

But then she'd asked something that Sarah found strange: Could she come, talk to her, maybe with her American friend?

A matter – she said – 'of some delicacy'. So here they were – first appointment of the day on a Monday morning which should have been basking in the warm aftermath of Saturday's School fête but which felt miserable and deflated.

"Did you ever get the cane, Jack?" Sarah said, trying to cheer herself up more than anything.

"Cane? You Brits are so primitive," said Jack. "When I was a kid, my Dad did remove his belt once. After I set off some fireworks in the school gym. Just took it off, and that was enough for me. Of course, in my day we did have God's watchful eyes on us as well."

Sarah laughed.

Jack tilted his head. Nodding to the secretary whose eyes were raised over her large glasses.

"Careful. It feels like we're in enough trouble already."

The door to reception opened, and a familiar figure entered: the infamous assistant head – Mrs Pynchon.

"Can I help you, Mrs Edwards? Is there anything wrong? With Daniel?"

Sarah looked up. Mrs Pynchon stood above her, face grim, owl-like eyes looking down as she held a clipboard under her arm.

Over two years of parents' evenings Sarah had learned that Mrs Pynchon had a reputation as a teacher to avoid, whether by parent or pupil. Daniel had been lucky to dodge her – but other parents had told of the joyless months their children had spent suffering in Pynchon's classroom.

"I'm here to see Mrs Harper," said Sarah. "And it's Ms, actually."

"Of *course*," said Mrs Pynchon, voice dripping, as if Sarah's status as a single mother was only to be expected given her obvious failings as a woman.

Sarah saw her heavy-lidded eyes swing sideways to alight on Jack. Now this would be interesting…

"And you are?"

"A friend," said Jack, smiling warmly at her.

"I'm sorry?" said Mrs Pynchon.

"No apology needed," said Jack graciously.

Jack interacting with the locals, thought Sarah. *Always fun to watch.*

She was just about to burst out laughing when fortunately the little light above Mrs Harper's door flicked from red to green.

The door opened and Cherringham's lone uniformed policeman emerged, donning his cap as he came out. Sarah smiled at him – her old friend Alan Rivers.

"Sarah – Jack," he nodded grimly and then he was gone.

What was Alan doing here? she thought.

"You can go in now Ms Edwards and Mr Brennan," said the secretary.

Sarah and Jack got up. Mrs Pynchon still stood, watching them, confused.

Whatever Mrs Harper's concern was – Sarah guessed – it hadn't been shared with the assistant head.

"Ah – parting is such sweet sorrow," said Jack to Mrs Pynchon with the slightest of bows as he followed Sarah into the head's office.

Too funny! Sarah didn't dare look over her shoulder to see Mrs Pynchon's expression – but surely, in all her years stalking the corridors of Cherringham Primary, nobody had dared to play her like that.

SARAH HAD NEVER been in Mrs Harper's office, but stories of it were legendary.

Books piled on the floor, the desk at sea, drowning under stacks of paper, a computer screen struggling to rise above the maelstrom.

And Mrs Harper herself... not the most stylish Cherringham resident.

Hair twirled and pinned back as if it could be dealt with later. A drab no-nonsense outfit of blouse and trousers completed the picture.

But her smile?

Sarah had seen Mrs Harper beam at the children putting on the Christmas play, or at a raucous music recital, or even just watching them run around at playtime.

That she loved those kids and this school was never in doubt.

Now, she looked up from her desk at Sarah, then Jack, as if their visit was an unannounced surprise. And that star smile was clearly missing today.

"Oh, sorry was just looking for —"

A brush at the desk as if magically some errant piece of paper could be made to appear.

"Was just… um, oh and —"

Whatever it was she'd been looking for, she had given up. "Please sit."

Two chairs faced Mrs Harper's desk and as Sarah sat down she noticed Jack scanning the room.

He's a good sport coming here, she thought. *With an amazing tolerance for village quaintness.* "Mrs Harper, this is —"

"I know. Mr Brennan, I —"

"Jack," he said.

Mrs Harper came from around the desk to shake his hand.

"I wanted to thank you personally – for the other day. Tending to poor Mr Brendl."

Jack looked over at Sarah. Neither had been sure what this was about. Now they were about to find out.

"I wish…" Jack said, "that it had turned out differently."

Mrs Harper looked away, turning to the windows, blinds rolled fully up, showing the empty school field which only days before had been filled with summer activity.

"We all do. Otto Brendl was a special man." She turned back. "He loved doing his shows, and the children – well you saw the crowd."

She took a breath. "He will be missed."

Sarah was tempted to ask the headmistress the reason for the meeting, the so-called 'matter of delicacy'. But she bided her time, thinking that the woman would come to the matter when she was ready. Finally Mrs Harper walked back to her chair and sat down.

"You know his history, don't you?"

Sarah saw Jack shake his head while she said, "No. Only that he came to Cherringham years ago."

The headmistress smiled. "I was just a new teacher then, and he was also new to the village, so I suppose I was always aware of him. The Berlin Wall had just come down – seems like only yesterday doesn't it? He was from East Germany you see. Whenever they showed the news coverage he used to say – 'look, that's me with a hammer and the long hair! Knocking down the Berlin Wall!' – but I don't think it was. A joke, you know? I think he just walked across the old border one day. Then got fed up in West Germany. Came here. He never talked much about growing up. He was an orphan, I seem to remember."

"Why Cherringham?" Jack said.

"I don't know. I think it's just where he happened to end up. Our little village. He got a job at the jewellers, and when the owner died, Mr Brendl took over the shop."

"And the shows?" Jack said. "Did he always do them?"

"No, not at first. He had these beautiful puppets – a gift from back home, apparently. He used to bring them in, show the children. Do little stories – German stories. Wonderful. But then, I suppose once he felt like he was really part of Cherringham, he built that stage himself, and started to do Punch and Judy. In the end it just became part of village life."

Sarah saw Jack look over. She had been around him enough to know when his questions were more than polite chit-chat. "Never married?" Jack said.

Did the headmistress harbour some feelings for Mr Brendl herself? Big age difference there, but Mrs Harper's fondness for the dead man felt so strong.

"No. He eventually became, um, friends with Jayne Reid. She runs the little knitting shop next door to his. They were so sweet together, acting as if nobody knew they were," a small smile, "an item. They'd dine out together, have tea together —"

"But they kept their own homes, never…?"

Mrs Harper nodded.

"Yes, she lived in her little flat above her shop, and Mr Brendl had his cottage, just outside the village."

Then Sarah saw Mrs Harper look out of the window. A cloud had cut off the sun over the field.

Sarah shot Jack a look, as if to say… *not sure what is happening here.*

And then the headmistress turned, took a breath, and the reason for the meeting became clear.

5.

A FAVOUR

"I'M TOTALLY USELESS at book-keeping. Records. All the things the education authorities want you to stay on top of."

That much – Sarah could see – was obvious.

"And at any school function, everyone participating has got to be 'in the system'. Any health issues, legal history, and all that. But with Mr Brendl, well, you know, he was an institution."

She gave the pile on her desk a desultory push.

"You mean you didn't do any of the checks?" said Sarah, barely able to hide her astonishment. "None at all?"

"I thought we had done – years ago. That's what Mr Brendl thought too. So I sort of... forgot about it. And then yesterday I came in – and couldn't find his file. And then I thought – oh maybe we didn't? So now —"

"You're worried that something might come out and damage the school?" Sarah said.

"Or my tenure here, at least. You may have guessed that there are plenty of people craving the position, and there have been reports before, papers not filed on time, silly things, you know."

Sarah could imagine the raptor-like Mrs Pynchon waiting in the wings to pounce on this office and put it *right*. She couldn't quite believe that Mrs Harper had been so negligent – especially in this day and age. But to lose this head teacher, that would indeed be a great loss.

"So, I don't know. I thought of you two. If there was anything I should have known about dear Mr Brendl, anything that might cause problems now…"

Again Jack looked at Sarah.

Not at all what they expected.

Mrs Harper looked from one to the other. Then Jack – as solid as an oak, with an answer that Sarah could have predicted – spoke. "I guess we could take a look."

Mrs Harper's face lightened a bit. "Would you? I can't thank you enough —"

Jack smiled. "Don't know what – if anything – we might find. But perhaps, if there was anything to be concerned about —"

"You know what they say! Forewarned is forearmed."

"Exactly," Jack said, still smiling.

The meeting seemed over, with the two of them having a case… sort of. But then Mrs Harper leaned in close, lowering her voice.

"One more thing. Mr Brendl's stage, his puppets, his little van. They're all still here. No next of kin – as far as I know. Eventually I imagine his estate – be that what it may – will go into probate. But perhaps best those things were returned. I don't suppose —"

"We could take them back?" Jack's words had to be reassuring. "Not a problem."

He turned to Sarah. "Perhaps I can follow you in Mr Brendl's van?" Then back to Mrs Harper. "You have the keys to his cottage?"

A nod. "Yes. They were with his puppets. I had the caretaker load everything back into his van this morning. You're sure you don't mind?"

Jack stood up.

"Don't even think about it. We'll do it now. And if you think it's okay, we'll talk to Ms Reid. Just to be sure there are no surprises for you about Mr Brendl."

Mrs Harper took Jack's right hand with both of hers and shook it hard.

"Thank you. For me, for my school, for the children – what we have here is too precious to lose."

Sarah came to her. "And the village knows that," she said.

A bigger smile from the head, then: "Right then, to the car park and I can get you started."

At the door, Jack paused.

"We saw Alan Rivers," he said. "I guess he was asking questions about Saturday?"

"Actually no," Mrs Harper replied. "Different thing entirely. We had a break-in last night. Someone ransacked the food stores. Cakes, biscuits. Made a right mess."

"Some kind of silly dare, I suppose," said Sarah.

"End of term hijinks – which today of all days I could do without," said the Head, for once unsmiling. "I wouldn't normally get the police involved – but Mrs Pynchon insisted."

And Mrs Harper led them out of the office, past the oh-so-curious eyes of the assistant head, and through the now quiet halls of the school.

JACK DROVE THE puppet van, thinking it must be odd for people to watch it go by and instead of seeing their beloved Otto Brendl, see him driving, oversized for the small van, his head grazing the ceiling.

He saw a switch that he guessed would turn on a speaker, music designed to signal that the puppeteer was nearby.

But now he drove in silence, thinking about what he had agreed to do.

He might have thought it nothing, simply dealing with returning

Brendl's puppets and maybe a little background work to reassure the teacher.

But there was one thing playing on his mind, something he hadn't yet mentioned to anyone, not even Sarah.

The matter of the tattoo.

Instinct's a funny thing, he thought. *We don't know where it comes from, but boy do we ever trust it.*

Ahead, he saw Sarah slow down and indicate to turn off the main road onto a narrow, single lane leading up into a wooded area.

Turning in, Jack hung back as the bushes and hedge – not as orderly as Jack had grown used to – made Sarah's car disappear around the hairpin twists and turns.

He came round one corner and just missed a young guy in jeans and waterproof jacket, who pressed himself back into the hedge.

Jack checked the mirror to make sure the man was okay – and he seemed all right, standing at the edge of the road, calmly watching the little van until Jack rounded the next curve.

THE RUTTED DIRT road made the puppet van bounce up and down. Jack heard the heavy pieces of the stage, stacked behind him, jump with each bump and indentation.

He hoped that the Punch and Judy puppets were securely fastened.

Should have checked that, he thought.

Then – a hundred yards ahead – a small cottage, girded by trees, overlooking a ravine.

All by itself.

He pulled up beside Sarah's car as they both got out to look at the cottage.

"KINDA ISOLATED," JACK said. "Wonder why he'd live way out here?"

Sarah looked out over rolling hills, the nearby farms, glimpses of the main road. But no question – Brendl was all on his own out here.

She turned to Jack.

"Must have liked his privacy. Or maybe, even after all these years he still didn't feel part of the village."

"Maybe. Let me open up the van and get the stuff out. Then – perhaps take a look around?"

"You think Mrs Harper might have something to worry about?"

"Who knows?"

She felt Jack hesitate – something else he was thinking but not saying? But he went to the garishly coloured van, opened the back, and began unloading the pieces of Brendl's stage set.

Sarah went to the front door, and a security light flashed on above her.

She held Brendl's key ring – so strange to have something so personal belonging to a dead man.

The front door had two locks, and she began the trial and error process of trying each key while Jack brought Brendl's props and stage set over.

"There's a big old basket in the back, buckled. Think it has Brendl's 'cast'. Any luck here?"

"Lots of keys."

Finally one went in, and she turned it.

"Got that open. Now…"

Sarah tried the same process on the lower lock.

"Pretty substantial locks," Jack said.

Sarah nodded, and pointed overhead. "And he has one of those motion detector lights. Came on soon as I stepped near."

Sarah got better at guessing which shape might fit the second lock, and she opened the heavy deadbolt. "Wonder if old Mr Brendl kept some jewellery here?" Jack said.

"That would explain all this."

As the last key found its home they entered the puppeteer's cottage. And despite having the keys and even though they were doing a favour, it felt – as they walked into the shadowy darkness – as if they were breaking in.

6.

COTTAGE SECRETS

SARAH HELPED JACK stack the stage pieces just inside the front door.

They probably had a proper place to be stored – but all of this would vanish sooner or later anyway.

With no heirs, Brendl's isolated getaway would be sold, his possessions as well.

"Want to bring the puppet case in?" she asked.

"Er – let's take a look around first."

In the shadows, she looked at him, surprised. "You mean search the place? I think Mrs Harper meant just do some digging into his background."

Jack seemed to pause. "Sarah. I saw something – when I opened Brendl's shirt."

And he told her about the tattoo, how he'd seen it before, decades ago on the shores of Brooklyn. On another dead body.

"What is it? What do you —"

"Not at all sure. I've sent an email to a friend at One Police Plaza. He worked the streets of Brighton back then."

"And?"

"No answer. It was the weekend. Should hear later today. Probably nothing."

Sarah nodded, and though it was definitely a sunny day she felt chilled.

"Okay – let's explore. But I'll be very surprised if we find anything."

And they began walking through the small cottage.

SARAH ENTERED THE tiny kitchen, shaded by a large tree outside, and looking gloomy and unused, just a lone upturned coffee cup in a rusty dish drainer.

Nothing attached to the old-fashioned fridge with magnets; no notes or reminders. And it looked as if it was the original ancient appliance from decades ago when Brendl had moved here.

Out of the corner of her eye, she saw a shadow flick across the kitchen window. She turned, thinking that maybe Jack had gone outside again – but there was nobody there. Then she heard a banging sound – and she froze.

There it was again. Close by.

She almost called out for Jack, the fear so quick and sudden. She walked over to the back door that led out of the kitchen. It was shut, but just outside, an outer storm-door flapped in the summer breeze coming off the nearby hills west of Cherringham.

Open. And outside – nobody.

And now – not from fear – she said, "Jack? Can you come here?"

The outer door flapped again, banging against its frame while she waited.

"Okay." Jack was crouched down looking at the door's handle and lock. He touched the wooden frame. "See? Scratched. Someone pried this open, then – here, the wood around the lock here, all chewed up?"

Sarah nodded.

"Based on what we saw out front, I doubt old Otto Brendl would leave the back door in such disrepair."

"Someone has broken in?"

"Looks that way. They were able to lock the kitchen door behind them, but this – they chewed up the wood too much."

"And what would they break in for?"

Jack stood up, and she saw him wearing a now-familiar lost-in-his-thoughts expression.

And Jack's thoughts usually led somewhere.

"I think," he turned to her, "the real question is — what did Brendl have that he was so concerned about? Why did he have multiple doors, locks, the lighting system? Did he keep jewels from the store here?"

"Perhaps some locals thought that. Broke in."

"Maybe. You see that guy back on the road just now?"

"Yes. You think something's odd there?"

"Not sure. Probably just a walker," said Jack, shrugging.

She could see that he wasn't convinced.

More ideas in play than a simple break-in at a dead man's cottage.

"Let's keep looking around. Head upstairs?"

Sarah nodded, and Jack led the way back inside.

BRENDL'S BEDROOM WAS simply furnished. A small four-poster bed, covered by a faded duvet with swirls of flowers, their colour long faded. A plain dresser with claw feet. A wooden chair.

It was a room almost devoid of personality, Sarah thought. Or a bedroom as someone might leave it... if it wasn't theirs.

Something odd about it.

She went over to the dresser, aware that they were doing more now than simply returning Brendl's Punch and Judy puppets. There had been no crime – yet here they were snooping around the old man's house, looking for something.

Sarah opened a drawer to see a foreign-language newspaper, dated a week ago.

But she could tell one thing: the newspaper wasn't in German. And now it was as if opening that drawer had allowed a secret part of Brendl's life to suddenly appear in the featureless room. She spread the paper on the bed as Jack stood beside her.

"Not in German, right? Do you know what language it is?"

"Something – I dunno – Eastern European. See this," he pointed to a word at the top. "*Bucharesti.* That's —"

"Romania. Dated last week too."

"Why would Mr Brendl have a Romanian newspaper? I mean, if he came from East Germany?"

"Good question."

As Sarah flipped through the paper and recognisable words and images leaped out... Obama... then a photo of Putin.

Jack looked around the otherwise characterless room.

"Nothing else here," he said.

"Seemed to be another room off the sitting room, possibly a cupboard. Worth a look?"

7.

MISSING TREASURES

DOWNSTAIRS, THEY WENT into the small sitting room and towards what looked like a large cupboard door. Sarah kept her ear cocked. Though they had a reason to be here, they had no right to be doing *this*.

The cupboard had a lock.

"Interesting," said Sarah.

Jack ran his finger over the surface of the lock. "This lock's all scratched up too. Someone tried to break in. Maybe they succeeded."

"Jack – you think we should call Alan?"

"In due time. Let's see what's behind… door number one. Have Brendl's keys handy?"

Sarah dug the key ring out of her jeans pocket and gave them to him. Jack began testing one key after the other until finally he found the right one. He gave it a turn...

THE DOOR OPENED with an appropriate creak. Jack stood back so that Sarah, who was using her phone as a torch, could go in first.

It was probably the one time she could have done without the chivalrous gesture.

She bent down – the entryway was low, just enough for the short Mr Brendl, but not Sarah. What she saw stopped her dead in her tracks.

This 'cupboard' was actually a room, and looking around she saw that it was girded by a series of empty cases, lined in black velvet, all tilted at an angle. Each case was three or four feet long, and each looked like a miniature coffin, the light from her phone casting an eerie glow that made the comparison even more apt.

Jack found the switch and with a click the room flooded with light, but it did little to dispel the funereal atmosphere in the cramped space.

"Wow," is all that Jack could say.

She turned to him. "He kept his puppets here."

Jack nodded. "And not just his Punch and Judy performers. Must have been a dozen other puppets *used* to be here."

"Whoever broke in must have taken them. But why take puppets?"

Jack went to each case, felt the plush black velvet, the perfect indentation matching each missing puppet. "Doesn't make sense. I expected a room of Rolexes. Tiaras. But missing dolls?"

"Now we call the police, right?"

He nodded. "Could be just what you said… locals break in, find these puppets – Brendl's 'treasure' – and take them, maybe figuring they're worth something."

"Could be," Sarah said.

Jack looked at her. "Not so convinced?"

She shook her head. "Why would Brendl go to all this trouble?"

"That's the question. Not sure where we go for the answer."

Sarah paused a moment. Then: "What about Jayne Reid? If Otto did have secrets, she might be the one who knows. Though right now all we have is an old man whose house has been burgled."

"Maybe. I'm thinking that I'd best find out about that tattoo.

NYC is waking up, weekend over. See what I can learn."

"But what about the puppets we brought? Put them back in here?"

Jack shook his head. "No. What if it was those Punch and Judy puppets that whoever broke in was looking for? I think for now I'll just keep them with me on the Goose. I'm sure the police and Mrs Harper would agree."

"Good idea," Sarah said. "I'll drop you back at the boat then pay a visit to Ms Reid."

She hesitated before leaving the room. "Jack – you really think there's something *here*, right?"

Jack took a breath as if weighing the question up. "Beginning to look that way to me."

And then the two of them walked out of the deserted room of empty puppet cases, leaving the door open.

ALAN SHOWED UP and once Jack had explained things to him, he agreed that it was best that Jack hold onto the Punch and Judy puppets for now. It was clear though that he felt it was probably just locals preying on the abandoned cottage of a dead old man.

Sarah thought that Alan looked harassed so she and Jack silently decided not to mention the newspaper or tattoo, at least until they knew more.

She dropped Jack off at his boat, helping him carry the basket with the surviving puppets inside.

"Be careful, Jack," she said, before she left. "As you said, could have been these puppets they were looking for – and now you have them."

He smiled at her concern, and she immediately felt silly considering the dangers he must have faced on the streets of New

York.

"I will. Call me as soon as you're done with Ms Reid?"

She nodded. Daniel was playing cricket up at the nets all day, Chloe had signed up to a drama workshop. Grace, her assistant, was hopefully managing things at her web studio – summer was slow anyway.

So, a good time to dig into Otto Brendl's life. And for once, Sarah really hoped she wasn't going to find anything.

8.

A WALK BY THE RIVER

SARAH HAD EXPECTED the proprietor of the 'Why Knot' knitting shop to be a little old lady, round and soft and sweet, wearing a knitted cardigan and almost certainly in a misery of mourning.

In fact, she was anything but – and Sarah had to contain her surprise when they finally met at the start of the river-walk down by Cherringham Bridge. Jayne Reid was in her early fifties, lean, sharp, in jeans and a runner's fleece, and Sarah realised that she recognised her from walking around the village.

Sarah had gone to 'Why Knot' and had found it closed. Next door, the shutters were also down on Otto Brendl's jeweller's shop. A little discreet asking around had turned up a mobile number, and Sarah had finally got through to Jayne.

Sarah's tentative suggestion that perhaps they could meet for a chat had turned into a brisk instruction to meet her 'in one hour precisely or not at all'. Jayne led a busy life it seemed and if Sarah was going to find out more about Otto Brendl she was going to have to pay the piper…

"I usually walk up as far as the old church and back," said Jayne after they'd made their introductions by the stile on the river path.

"Lovely," said Sarah.

"Good," said Jayne, striding ahead along the river bank.

Sarah caught up – and tried to figure out her tactics.

She'd always found that walking together was a good way to interview someone. Plenty of time to think and there were no awkward silences. Distractions, possibilities of finding shared interests, ways of changing the subject if one particular direction got awkward.

And here in the meadows opposite the residential moorings, on a warm summer's afternoon, under a blue sky, there should be no shortage of things to talk about. The river was busy with little boats, fishermen and kids in kayaks.

All she had to do was get Jayne talking, get the information flowing.

"You're sure you don't mind me asking you about Mr Brendl?" she said, keeping step with Jayne's brisk, no-nonsense pace.

"That depends upon the questions."

"We're just trying to get a sense of his background so that we can —"

"— get Mrs Harper off the hook," said Jayne. "That's really what this is about, isn't it?"

"Sorry?"

Sarah hadn't expected *that* comment.

"Oh come on, Sarah, I wasn't born yesterday," said Jayne. "Otto never got round to those ridiculous checks and now instead of people remembering him for his charity work, that bloody stupid woman is going to pollute his reputation by sending you and your American —"

Jayne Reid stopped dead and spun round, to point across the river towards Jack's boat, moored just thirty yards away.

38

"That where he lives, isn't it?" she said, as if accusing Sarah of some kind of crime.

Sarah nodded.

"I suppose he's watching me through binoculars," said Jayne, shaking her head. "So, where was I? Yes – my good friend dies and minutes later I'm being questioned by two bloody amateur detectives trying to dig up dirt."

"Ms Reid, that's not true. We're just trying to —"

"For God's sake call me 'Jayne', will you," she said, spinning on her heels and carrying on up the footpath. "Ms? Ms? Ridiculous form of address!"

Sarah hurried along behind her to catch up. This wasn't going at all the way she'd imagined – she needed to change tack and fast.

"I'm not sure if you know, but somebody broke into Mr Brendl's house over the weekend and stole his puppets."

Jayne stopped so suddenly that Sarah nearly bumped into her.

"What? No, I didn't," she said, her brow furrowed in anger. "How do *you* know? And why wasn't I told?"

"We only found out this morning. Jack and I took the Punch and Judy back to his cottage and —"

"So *you've* got his keys? I don't believe this."

"The keys were actually in the little theatre, so Mrs Harper —"

"I asked at the hospital for them; they wouldn't give them to me —"

"I'm sure that's only because they didn't have them —"

"I thought they were just being bloody-minded, I didn't expect the school to be in on it too."

Sarah realised that Jayne was still in shock at Otto Brendl's death – somehow she was going to have to calm her down.

"I'm sure Mrs Harper intended to pass the keys onto you," she said.

"Oh God, back to Mrs Harper again – I really don't want to talk about that woman – okay?"

"Of course."

"Come on," said Jayne, striding off once more down the river path.

Sarah watched her marching away and thought:

I could just leave this for now. Catch her later. Take a breather. Grab a cuppa over at Jack's boat.

But something – some instinct – told her that there might never be a better time to question Jayne Reid.

She hurried after her.

TEN MINUTES OF fast walking had passed without a word between them.

Sarah had decided to let Jayne Reid stew for a while. In silence they'd followed the slow winding shape of the river path upstream, occasionally crossing stiles or footbridges over small brooks. Up here there were fewer pleasure boats and holidaymakers. The meadows turned to pasture and Sarah kept an eye on groups of inquisitive cows as they walked by them.

On any other day this would be a lovely walk, she thought.

But she was determined not to give in.

Eventually the path curved in across the meadow and Sarah saw they were close to the old church, which stood on a raised mound just a few hundred yards from the Thames.

Ahead of her, Jayne had reached the dry stone wall which surrounded the churchyard. She pushed the ancient wooden gate and held it open for Sarah.

"I haven't been here for years," said Sarah.

"We – I – come here every day," said Jayne over her shoulder, striding up the stone path to the church entrance.

Sarah paused and took in the familiar view.

St Paul's Church, Ingleston.

When she was a teenager she and her friends used to come up here, drink cider in the graveyard and scare each other half to death.

In truth, it had always been, to her, the most peaceful, romantic place. She'd even written an essay about it as a local history project.

The church had once been at the heart of Ingleston, she remembered – but the village had been decimated during the Black Death. The fields all around were dotted with grassy mounds, under which slept the grim remains of the abandoned cottages and barns.

"Come on," said Jayne, holding the heavy church door open. Sarah walked up the church path, past ancient gravestones, marked with skulls and gothic texts.

Through the open church door, she could see only darkness. She crossed the threshold.

9.

DOOM

AFTER THE BRIGHT sunlight, it took a few seconds for Sarah's eyes to adjust. She looked around. The church was empty. It looked just as it had done twenty years ago.

It probably hasn't changed for hundreds of years, she thought.

Instead of the modern plastic chairs which filled most churches these days, here there were seventeenth-century box pews. And on the crumbling walls there were faded paintings which must go back more than a thousand years, depicting biblical scenes.

As Sarah followed Jayne through the church, her footsteps echoed on the smooth, worn flagstones.

Eventually Jayne stopped at the altar and sat on a bench. Sarah joined her and waited. The air was cool. Outside, Sarah could hear birdsong and the occasional playful shouts from children on the river.

"You see the 'Doom'?" said Jayne, nodding to the faded painting on the East wall.

"Doom?" asked Sarah.

"Judgement Day. Right there. Christ separating those who will go to Heaven, from those who will go straight to Hell."

Sarah looked at the wall and suddenly remembered how, as a teenager, she'd been fascinated by the details in this graphic image of Hell, the ingenious tortures imagined by the medieval painter.

"This was Otto's favourite place," said Jayne eventually. "In the whole world, he said."

"Was he religious?" said Sarah, sensing that Jayne was ready to talk.

"No, not now."

"But once?"

"As a child in Germany – yes, I think so." She took a breath. "We didn't talk about that."

"He grew up there?"

Was there a bit of hesitation?

"In Erfurt. What used to be East Germany."

"But he never went back?" said Sarah.

"He hated it. He was an orphan. It was communism. Would you go back?"

Sarah knew she had to keep this conversation going.

"He has no next of kin?" she said.

"No."

"He never talked about his family?"

"Are you listening? He grew up in an institution."

"So, Jayne. You and Otto…" Sarah groped for the right word. "Were you…?"

Dangerous ground here.

"We were very close," said Jayne, turning and looking directly at Sarah. "Is that enough for you?"

Sarah nodded and changed the subject.

"Where did he learn to do puppetry? In Germany?" she said.

"I don't know," said Jayne. "I think so. When we first met, he showed me his Kasperletheater. Very old, and those classic German puppets… so beautiful."

"He kept them in special cases," said Sarah, coaxing.

"Yes," said Jayne. "They were worth a fortune."

"Really? Did anyone else know about them?"

43

Sarah spoke softly. She sensed that Jayne's anger was beginning to dissolve, sitting here in the cool air of the church.

"People in the trade, I suppose," said Jayne. "Otto bought and sold puppets online, you see. Never his most precious ones, of course. But others he ordered from all over Europe and then sold on."

"And you don't know who might have broken into his house and stolen them?"

"Oh, but I do," said Jayne, turning to Sarah as if her question hardly needed asking.

Sarah blinked in surprise.

"Who?"

"Krause, of course."

"Krause?"

"'The Puppet King' he calls himself."

"Is he local?"

"He's got a unit on an estate outside Chipping Norton. Full of party crap."

"But he sells puppets too?"

"He does shows. Bad Punch and Judy shows. Or junk with themed puppets. Horrible things – ripped off from American cartoons."

"And you think he stole Otto's puppets?"

"Krause *hated* Otto. Tried to put him out of business."

"Why?" said Sarah.

"He was jealous, of course," said Jayne. "Otto's puppets were handmade, special. He did shows the old-fashioned way. The children loved him."

Jayne sniffed the air.

"Krause was a hack. Otto was an artist."

"SO, KRAUSE SAW Otto as a threat?"

"Of course," said Jayne. "It was all about money for him! But also he wanted Otto's puppets so he could sell them, had some secret buyers lined up. He offered Otto thousands. Every week he phoned. Kept coming into the jewellers, making trouble, trying to force Otto to sell. Otto told him where to go. Nicely, of course. Otto was always too nice."

For a second Sarah wondered what she was doing here.

The plan had been just to make sure there was nothing untoward in Otto Brendl's life that could come back to haunt Mrs Harper. But now, it seemed she was tumbling into a bizarre puppet war...

"Do you have any proof of all this? Anything we could talk to the police about?"

"I don't need *proof*," said Jayne, and Sarah could see her anger flash across her face.

Another sniff. Jayne Reid was a force to be reckoned with.

"Krause is evil. He did it. He stole Otto's puppets. End of story."

10.

THE PUPPET KING

"IN YOUR BASKET, Riley," said Jack. "You know the deal."

Riley gave Jack his most pleading expression, then turned, whining, and slouched down the wheelhouse steps into the saloon.

In the time that he and the Springer Spaniel had lived together on the Grey Goose, Jack had learned to ignore these looks – but he never liked to be parted from his dog for long.

He padlocked the wheelhouse and walked the short gangway to the river bank.

"Gonna be a scorcher, Jack!" came a voice from the next but one barge. Jack squinted against the bright early morning sun. There in a deckchair on the fore-deck of the old Magnolia was Ray Stroud, shirt off, tin mug of tea in one hand, a roll-up cigarette in the other.

Maybe it was tea. That the cigarette was tobacco was more doubtful.

As far as Jack could tell, Ray was the only genuine hippy left in the Cotswolds and a handy 'in' to the shadier activities of the area. Handy too, when Jack needed help on the boat – though the price was often a hangover the next day.

"Yep, warming up nicely," said Jack as he headed down the riverbank towards the old bridge car park. "You up to much today?"

"Might tickle a few trout this arvo," said Ray chewing on the roll-up that was glued to the corner of his mouth. "Then it's happy hour down the Ploughman's. Suppose I'll have to go. Can't let them down now, can I?"

"I'm sure you can't," said Jack grinning.

Ray spat into the river.

"See you locked up there, Jack."

"Always do," said Jack, pausing.

This wasn't idle chatter. He could see Ray hesitating, as if he had something to share. Then:

"Only I heard there was a fella asking after you last night, up at Iron Wharf."

"Oh yeah?"

"So I hear," said Ray. "Asking which of these boats might be yours."

"Really? I'm obliged to you for the information, Ray."

"'s what neighbours are for."

"And… don't suppose you heard any more?"

Ray pulled himself up from the deckchair and tossed the dregs of his cup into the river.

Then he crossed the deck to be nearer to Jack.

Jack edged closer to the barge – he knew that any exchange of information with Ray had to be treated seriously, respectfully.

"What I heard was… that this fella doing the enquiring was a young'un. Had an accent. Russian, or somethin' – they reckoned."

"Uh-huh," said Jack taking this in.

"And what with you being American, Jack – well you'll know what that means."

"I surely do," said Jack, not knowing at *all* what that meant.

Jack stared at Ray, who nodded slowly, then tapped his nose.

"Good to be prepared, eh?" he said then turned on his heels and went back to his deckchair.

"How true. And thanks Ray."

47

Jack too turned – and carried on down the river bank past the other moored boats and barges.

On any other day, he might have treated Ray's little chat as a symptom of overheated local imaginings, fuelled by whatever.

But right now there were thin connections forming in the back of his mind, threads of ideas, wisps of coincidence that he couldn't ignore. *And I don't believe in coincidence*, he thought.

The tattoo on Brendl's chest. Brighton Beach. East European gangs. And now a young Russian.

That man on the road near Brendl's place. A walker? A stranger? What was he doing on that road? It went nowhere. Only to Brendl's cottage…

And Krause, the man that Sarah had called him about, the man he was on his way to meet this morning over in Chipping Norton.

The Puppet King.

All these disconnected threads.

What did all this have to do with the sad death of an old man at an English summer fête?

ON THE EARLY morning empty roads, it only took Jack around twenty minutes to get to Chipping Norton – and he relished driving the Healey Sprite in the sunshine, wind blowing.

The little sports car flew like a fire-cracker up and down the Cotswold hills and, with the top down, it reminded him of some crazy vacation trips in his youth along the Pacific Coast Highway.

Sarah had filled him in on her chat with Jayne Reid – and now he thought about it, he knew he'd seen Jayne and Brendl more than once in the past year on the meadows walking together along the river.

The industrial estate sat half a mile short of the town and, as he pulled off the main road and drew in, he was struck how all these little English towns seemed to have identical, scruffy little work units on their outskirts.

He drove slowly, inspecting each one – dog food distributor, bathrooms, pizza bases, tyres, tiles, furniture strippers, and then – how could anyone miss it…

FunLand!

Single storey, glass-fronted, garish colours, neon signs, balloons – and three people dressed as vegetables sitting on a bench having a smoke. Jack pulled up right in front of them.

As he got out of the car, the carrot and the onion ignored him. The pod of peas gave him a cursory nod.

Par for the course, he thought. *If it's a cigarette break, the customers can go hang.*

Jack went in and paused for a moment just behind the sliding doors.

Rows and rows of party gear stretched away to the back of the cavernous warehouse, each line individually themed. He could see Irish, Cowboy, Wizard, Superhero, Fairy…

Party music blared out of walls, balloons swung in the air and everywhere he could see signs telling him to 'Have Fun, you're in FunLand!'

In the back of the store, a thick black curtain barred the way to 'The Magician's Cave – Amazing Tricks and Illusions!'

Off to the right of the 'cave', a Punch and Judy stall. But this was nothing like the one he'd returned to Otto Brendl's house.

This one was decked out like Times Square on New Year's Eve, and instead of the old familiar characters, two superheroes were propped up, slugging it out. Neon lights flickered inside it and a soundtrack of looped explosions and guitars made the little theatre vibrate.

A placard next to the theatre said – 'Punch is dead – long live

Robot-man!'

So this was what Otto Brendl was up against. The Puppet King.

Jack shook his head in sad acceptance: change comes — dealing with it is hard.

He looked around.

As far as he could tell, he was the only customer. He went to the checkout. A plump girl dressed as a fairy sat texting on a stool.

"Hi. I'm here to meet Mr Krause."

The girl looked up and stared. Then, with a sigh, she put down her phone, picked up a microphone on a stand and bellowed into it:

"Mr *Krause* – to the tills! Mr Krause to the tills!"

The words boomed out over the PA.

Jack smiled at her. Least she didn't have to dress up as a vegetable. She put the microphone down and without looking at him again, picked up her phone and continued her zombie-like texting.

Jack waited.

Then Mr Krause appeared from an office at the side of the store, eyes wide as if he had been suddenly awakened.

And the way he looked was a surprise to Jack.

From Sarah's account of her little chat with Jayne, anything short of horns, a tail and matching goat's feet would have been a let-down. In fact, Mr Krause was a cheery middle-aged man with an open face. He greeted Jack with a big handshake, acting more like a Texan mayor campaigning for re-election.

"Mr *Brennan*! Pleasure to meet you!"

"Mr Krause —"

"Max, please, to all my friends!"

Suddenly we're friends...

"Jack."

Jack watched as Krause reached across and grasped the side of the Robot-man theatre.

"Seen this? Pretty cool huh?" he said with a big grin. "I do all the shows myself."

"Schools, parties – summer fêtes huh?"

"Everywhere and anywhere!" said the puppeteer. "The kids love it. We run the sound and lighting effects off a laptop. Big lights. Full surround sound. Very modern."

He leaned close to Jack, grin widening. Maybe some horns were now beginning to appear... "Scares the shit out of the mums, I can tell you!"

"I bet."

"Who wants truncheons and sausages? Thank God we don't live in that silly world anymore."

Jack looked at Max Krause's beaming face: right or wrong, the guy was certainly passionate about what he was selling.

"You want to look round the store, pick up some party treats? We got an adult section – sexy, sexy – don't worry, I won't tell a soul!"

"Maybe not this time, Max, I'm kinda pressed for time – you know?"

"No problem! Summer days like this don't come here often. No doubt we won't see many people in the store today." The smile faded a bit. "Shall we go into the office?"

Jack followed him to the office and stopped just feet into the room. Another surprise...

"Quite a sight, huh?" said Max. "My real life's work."

Jack scanned the room. There were special racks on every wall, and on each rack hung puppets. But not the cheap puppets he'd just seen in the shop.

No, these were old, weathered antiques, in rich silk costumes, oriental fabrics: old men, children, witches, kings, emperors, queens, mythical characters, nymphs, tigers, exotic birds.

A museum-worthy collection.

"Wow," said Jack. "But what you said out there..."

"Out there – I'm a *salesman*, Jack. And that stuff is my living."

"And this?"

"Oh this – this is different. This is my love."

Jack nodded, realising that nothing in this case was going to be as clear cut as it had seemed.

Krause sat down in a leather chair behind his desk and signalled to Jack to sit opposite him.

"So Max—" said Jack, leaning forward. "You know why I'm here?"

"Sure," said Max. "Somebody stole Otto Brendl's puppets and you think that somebody is me."

"No, I don't think that – yet. But it has been suggested to me that you are a likely suspect."

"You know something?" said Max. "I'd be disappointed if I wasn't the *most* likely suspect!"

Jack laughed. He couldn't help it.

He'd met guys like this before in New York. They played the game – and it was a game he knew well. One he enjoyed – a kind of 'catch me if you can'.

"Go on," he said.

"Let's face it – there's me, Otto and about two other guys in the whole damn country who know the value of those puppets. And the other two are idiots who probably haven't been out of their holes in the ground for weeks."

"So you don't deny you wanted them?"

"Deny? Why use that word? Deny! That's a terrible word. Let's say 'admit' – okay? I *admit* I wanted Otto's puppets. They're amazing. So rare. Baroque Czech puppets, eighteenth-century Kasperles from Germany, Gretels – beautiful Gretels – he had Guignols – you know he even had Romanian Magi – three of them, untouched, original…"

Jack watched as Max seemed to lose himself in the visions of Otto's collection.

"So yes, I wanted them," he said, coming down. "But did I steal them? No."

"So who did?" said Jack. "I mean – you're in the business – you'd know, wouldn't you?"

"Whoever stole them knew that Otto had just died – knew that a break-in was possible."

"That hardly narrows it down."

"It does a little," said Max, growing more serious. "The bastard didn't have any friends."

"Oh really? From what I hear he was very popular," said Jack.

"Not the same thing though, is it? Sure, the kids liked him. Not as much as they like me and my show, of course. But generally, they liked him. But he was a loner, wouldn't even talk to me about selling any of his collection!"

"Wouldn't that come with the territory?" said Jack.

"How do you mean?" said Max, clearly confused.

"You know – growing up in an orphanage. Living alone in East Germany, coming here on his own."

Max laughed.

"You've got something wrong there, Jack. Sorry! Otto Brendl wasn't German."

Jack felt the sands shifting in this investigation…

"According to the one person who knew him well, he grew up in Erfurt."

"That's what he said, huh? Funny. You know, I never understood why he bad-mouthed me so much. But now – of course – it's obvious."

"What do you mean?"

"*I'm* German, Jack. My family comes from Weimar. Erfurt is just a few miles away. I have been there many, many times. A beautiful city by the way – you must visit. And I can tell you categorically Otto Brendl did not come from Erfurt. In fact, I doubt very much he was even born in Germany."

"So where…?"

"From his accent – to the East, Jack. To the East, for sure."

And Jack sat back in his office chair, thinking fast.

"Romania…?" he said softly, as much to himself as to Max Krause.

"Those countries. All of them under the boot of Mother Russia. Could be Romania. Could be any of them. But German? 'Herr' Brendl was a man who surely told many lies, and that was one."

Jack looked at the puppets, hanging from the wall like a medieval rogues' gallery, eyes wide, as if they were hanging on every word.

Creepy.

"Other secrets?"

"How did he get those puppets? Some of them priceless. Not cheap at all. Never gave me a straight answer."

Jack looked right at Krause. A suspicious man, someone who clearly wanted those puppets too.

And someone who didn't like old Brendl at all.

For now those were just suspicions.

"Max, I need to go. This has been… quite illuminating."

The ghost of a smile returned to Krause's face. "Sure you don't want to look around, pick up a gag, check out our 'adult' wing?"

"You are too kind." Jack started to turn.

Then – a little trick he stole from a great, albeit fictional, detective on TV.

"One thing – I may have more questions. So, I might be back."

Max's smile faded.

Just the effect I'm looking for, Jack thought.

Krause nodded. Then: "Sure."

And Jack smiled back, walking out of the office, knowing that the proprietor of FunLand – for some still unknown reason – wasn't happy at the thought of a return visit.

11.

THE TATTOO

BEFORE HE GOT onto the road, and left Chipping Norton, Jack called Sarah and arranged to meet at Huffington's to compare notes.

Though still warm enough with the top down, off to the east the English weather was acting true to form, with grey clouds gathering, ready for an assault on the Cotswolds.

In a way, he liked that changeability. Mood-wise, Jack realised that it suited him.

He had BBC Radio Gloucestershire on as he drove – and that was another thing he had grown used to, becoming interested in the local political stories.

The accents, the tone of the reporting, all starting to seem normal now that he had left behind NYC's in-your-face twenty-four/seven newscasts and sports stations.

Sports. An obsession everywhere, even though the games change.

Though when he went back to New York, he did want to be sure to catch a game in CitiField before the Mets were once again – most likely – banished from any World Series hopes.

Get a hot dog with everything. Chill, sautéed onions, mustard, relish. An icy, cold beer.

Yeah...

There were definitely some things he missed.

He hit the dual carriageway that led south, weaving its way back to Cherringham, when his phone – sitting on the seat beside him – chirped.

He picked it up, answered. Might be hard to hear with the wind whipping, so he held it close.

"Hello?"

"Jack – Eddie Morgan. How you doing, you old bastard?"

And Jack laughed, hearing the voice of his old friend and fellow detective, still working the desks at One Police Plaza. For a few minutes they shared news and talked about their families.

Jack left out anything about his amateur detective work. Eddie was a by-the-book detective, a lifer who wouldn't find anything like that at all appropriate.

He learned news of Eddie's eldest child, who taught Middle School and whose wife was expecting their first child in November.

Eddie's pride was immense.

Then, more quickly, just a few words about Eddie's youngest, a troubled boy who Eddie always struggled to know how to deal with.

Life is never a clean and clear ride for anyone, thought Jack.

He told Eddie about Cherringham – his boat, the fishing, the martinis.

Then: "Thought you'd be back in a flash. Jack Brennan, living in a quiet English village, away from the crime and grime of the city? No way."

Not exactly away from crime, Jack thought.

"So Jack, that thing you sent me. That tattoo? You're right – we did see that pop up when working the mobs in Brighton."

Back in the nineties, Brighton had become an outpost for thousands of Russian and East European émigrés. Flashy clubs sprung up, vodka on ice, caviar that you could get nowhere else.

And as mobs are wont to do, there were shakedowns. Rackets. And people who suddenly *disappeared*. Took a while to get that under control.

"Some of the guys who showed up dead had the same tattoo. We had thought maybe it was gang-related. So I did some research for you."

A sign ahead indicated the narrow road that would lead to the north end of Cherringham. Even more twisty, Jack would need to slow down.

"Go on, Eddie."

"Sure, but Jack —"

Eddie was a savvy cop.

"What's this about, hmm? Where did you see this tattoo? And —" a small laugh, "— what the hell is it doing in England?"

"Eddie – would you believe me if I told you it has to do with a kindly old puppet master having a fatal heart attack? Just – colour me curious."

For a moment, Eddie said nothing.

"This puppet master. This kindly old dead guy. I'm guessing he's Romanian?"

Jack's turn to pause. Eddie had turned serious, the voice less 'old-friends' now, more professional, more… concerned.

"It appears that way."

"Right. Makes sense. Okay, so here's what we know about vulture tattoos, Jack."

And for the next few minutes taking those hedge-lined curves slowly, Jack just listened.

SARAH SAT AT a back table at Huffington's nursing a cup of tea.

Jack was due any minute, and the café was quiet in the gap between lunch and the gaggle that showed up for teatime.

"Anything else, Sarah?" Doris, a Huffington's institution, asked her. She had to be well into her sixties, yet she wore the black-and-white uniform of a Huffington member of staff like it was couture, and her mane of silver hair added to the overall effect of gran gone glam.

"No thanks," Sarah said, smiling. "Waiting for someone."

A big smile from Doris.

What's it like to spend your life working in a place like this? Sarah wondered.

The routine the same, the people the same – God, even the menu probably unchanged.

On one hand, it has to be reassuring; the constancy, watching kids grow up, seeing some move from the village, sharing the joys of offspring wed and the sadness of an old timer whose teatimes were done.

There are worse places to be.

The bell over the door trilled, and she looked up to see Jack, who quickly scanned the near-empty café and hurried over.

"Sorry. I didn't forget the time but that road back there? Suddenly a work crew had it down to one lane."

"They do that. You're lucky you didn't get diverted."

Jack smiled. "Would have tested my not in-depth knowledge of the roads around here."

"You *could* get a navigation system."

"Right. Not sure I'm ready for someone with an English accent telling me how and where to turn."

And Sarah grinned at that.

Doris appeared at Jack's shoulder, probably intrigued by an older gentleman meeting a younger single mum. But then, Doris would have heard the stories. Of who Jack was and what they had been up to.

"Anything for you, Jack?"

Jack looked up and smiled. "Why Doris, I believe so. How about a cup of English Breakfast, and a few of those shortbread cook – um, biscuits?"

Jack's mid-course correction to his order brought a smile to Doris. Sarah made a note to herself – *should have known Jack would be on first-name terms in here…*

"Coming right up."

Then Jack turned back to Sarah. "So – you want to hear about my little outing this morning?"

She could tell from the tone in Jack's voice that he was taking this rooting around Otto Brendl's life seriously – and perhaps he'd learned something in his visit with Max Krause.

The tea appeared.

"Thanks." Then: "Do tell."

And Jack described his visit to FunLand.

SARAH STARTED LAUGHING.

"Really? He actually had one of those…" she lowered her voice, "adult-only areas?"

"Yes, 'sexy, sexy' as he described it to me."

Another laugh. "If you like rubber products."

And Jack laughed at that.

"I don't suppose you actually went in —"

"Oh, I was tempted. Who could resist? Plus he had a nice selection of plastic vomit and other items perfect for your next lawn party."

Sarah shook her head. "Unbelievable."

Then Jack – as was his way, held the smile a bit, as he shifted gears.

And told her that Otto Brendl had a secret: that he wasn't German, at least according to Krause.

"Eastern Europe? You're kidding," said Sarah. "But he told Jayne all about his childhood in Erfurt."

"Krause was pretty insistent," said Jack. "Plus – on the way back my friend Eddie called from New York."

Jack took a bite of one of the shortbreads, and gestured at the batch towards Sarah. She took one, dipped it into her cooling tea, and bit off the soggy end.

"He recognised the tattoo?"

Jack nodded, face set. He looked around, their table off by itself. Still he lowered his voice.

"Sure did," said Jack. "Brighton beach. In the early nineties – just like I thought. So he did a bit of asking around – and he came up with a country. Romania."

"Romania?" said Sarah, coming to terms with the fact that Otto Brendl was not the man he had pretended to be.

"Yep," said Jack. "But here's the weird thing. Eddie tried to find out more – but nobody wanted to know. Mentioned the tattoo in a couple of Romanian cafés and people clammed up. He says it's not a drugs thing. He thinks it's politics."

Jack leaned in a bit closer.

"So here's the real question, Sarah. If Otto Brendl was really Romanian, why did he pretend to be German? Why did he come here, with a false identity, on his own? Why all by himself?"

Sarah looked away.

Thinking: there were things she could do. Anything was searchable, and with this information, she could do some digging.

"I can do some hunting, Jack. We'll know when he came here. I can search databanks, check Interpol for missing persons… I'll get Grace onto it – we're pretty quiet in the office. Records like that, they have to be somewhere online."

"I was hoping you'd say that."

"But there's something else we can do. Right now."

Jack raised his eyebrows, not following.

Sarah filled in the gap.

"Just *how* good was Otto at keeping secrets?"

"Hmm?"

"Did he keep his secret from everyone?"

Jack nodded.

"Jayne Reid."

"Exactly," she said. "I think it's time we paid her another visit – don't you?"

And with that she took Jack's last biscuit and stood up.

"Hey," said Jack. "That was mine."

"Got to be quick to catch me, Jack," she said. "And joking aside – this afternoon is piling up for me. Not only have I got to do a food shop but I've also got to make up a costume for Chloe *and* wash Daniel's cricket whites and have them dry by morning."

"The life of a single mum, hmm?" said Jack gesturing to Doris that he'd left cash on the table.

"Tell me about it," said Sarah, heading through the teatime crowd to the door.

12.

THE FUGITIVE

HALFWAY DOWN THE High Street, Sarah stopped.

"Oh no! I don't believe it," she said, turning to Jack. "Look."

Jack followed her gaze as she pointed at the little shop on the other side of the road.

"What's up?" said Jack following her gaze.

"Costco is closed. Which means when we're done with Jayne, I'm going to have get in the car and drive out to the supermarket for the kids' supper."

"Kinda odd – just being closed in the middle of the afternoon," said Jack.

"Been a robbery, hasn't there," said a voice next to them. Jack turned. A roundish woman in her thirties pushing a double buggy had joined them. Jack caught an exasperated roll of eyes from Sarah. He figured the woman was one of the army of mums that Sarah knew in the village.

"Hi Angela," she said.

"I've been waiting an hour for them to open," said Angela. "It was only a break-in, you'd think it was a bank-job or something the way your mate Alan's playing Sherlock bleedin' Holmes in there."

Jack noticed the little police car parked up outside the store: through the window he could just see the figure of PC Rivers talking to the owner.

"Someone filled a bag, did a runner out the back," said Angela. "Doesn't surprise me, the prices he charges. I mean, how are we supposed to —"

"Terribly sorry Angela – got to dash," said Sarah, surprising Jack with the speed she moved away down the High Street.

"Well," said Angela. "Don't mind me…"

"Nice to meet you, Angela," called Jack as he headed off to catch up with his fellow detective.

'WHY KNOT' WAS down a little alleyway off the High Street which Sarah jokingly called 'Cherringham's medieval quarter'. Jack knew it from the nearby bookshop and a terrific deli that he liked – he realised he'd walked past 'Why Knot' a hundred times without ever really noticing it.

He'd also hardly noticed the old-fashioned jeweller's next door, which now stood closed and shuttered.

The wool shop was brightly lit, but looked empty. Sarah pushed open the door and Jack followed. The place probably had hardly changed in fifty years: racks of wool, stands of knitting needles, trays of buttons and piles of patterns.

A tall, intelligent-looking woman emerged through floral curtains that masked a storage area.

"Can I help —" she said. "Oh, it's *you*."

"Hello Jayne," said Sarah. "I hope you don't mind, we had some more questions about Otto."

Jack watched Jayne Reid sizing him up. He smiled at her.

"I've told you everything I know," said Jayne, ignoring him. "Bringing your American friend along isn't going to change that."

"I'm afraid what we have to tell you *will* change things," said Jack, watching her closely.

"Oh, I very much doubt that," said Jayne confidently.

Jack saw Sarah catch his eye – he could tell she wanted to run with this. He nodded at her, their short-hand working together as good now as any of the partners he'd had back in New York.

"Jayne, we've found out some things about Otto which – to be honest – we don't understand," said Sarah. "And we thought you might be able to clear them up."

Jack could see a tell-tale flicker of concern move across Jayne Reid's face.

She knows something... he thought, and watched intently as Sarah told Jayne of his visit to the rival puppeteer and of Krause's denials of anything to do with the puppets' theft. Then he mentioned Krause's assertion that Otto was not German.

At this Jayne grunted.

"Krause!" she said, through gritted teeth. "That bastard would lie about anything – especially about Otto! Is this what you've both come here to tell me?"

Jack watched as she walked to the shop door and opened it wide.

"Get out, or I'll call the police," she said.

Instead of leaving, Jack went to the corner of the shop, pulled out a fold-up chair and sat on it.

"You really don't want to do that Jayne," he said patiently. "You see my police contacts back in New York tell me that Otto was Romanian, and the tattoo he had on his side, you know – the vulture..."

Jack could see from Jayne's expression that she knew exactly what he was talking about. The trick here, the trick of teasing the truth out of this woman, was not to reveal how little he and Sarah actually knew.

"Yes, you know the tattoo, don't you?" he said. "Well, they told me how *important* that tattoo was. But you know that too, don't you?

You talked to Otto about the tattoo and he explained it."

He smiled at her – and that seemed to break the spell that held all three of them motionless.

"All right," she said. "I'll tell you what I know. But I don't want it spread around – you understand?"

He watched as she shut the door and came and sat next to him. It was as if she had surrendered.

He caught Sarah's eye – she turned the sign on the door to 'closed', flicked the latch, then pulled another chair out and sat close to them.

"OTTO WAS THE kindest man I ever met," said Jayne Reid. "Old-fashioned – he always opened the door for me. Such a gentleman. But in truth, until he came here, he had a terrible, terrible life."

Sarah watched silently, not wanting to distract Jayne from her story, listening intently to every word.

"You are right. He was Romanian. His family stood up to the Ceauşescu regime – you know they were the Communist party that ran the country for years? So evil. Otto's father was in the opposition. He was executed. So Otto took up the cause – *that's* why he had that tattoo. He told me it was a secret sign for the revolution. But he was captured and tortured. By the Secret Police. The Securitate. You know of them?"

"I've read about them," said Jack. "They were about as bad as you could get. Took their methodology from the KGB. But even more brutal. Cross their paths and you disappeared. I remember after the Communists fell, all the truth came out – mass assassinations, torture, you name it."

"Otto never liked to talk about it. But I pieced together what happened to him. After they killed Ceauşescu, he was released from prison. He thought everything was going to be wonderful. But those people who had been in the Securitate, they wanted revenge. They were like mad men – they went after everybody who had crossed them. They hunted down the rest of Otto's family and killed them. Then they came after him. So, in 1989 he fled to Germany."

"To Erfurt," said Sarah.

"Yes," said Jayne. "That part was true. But he only stayed long enough to get a new identity. Then he came here."

"But all these years later – why didn't he just own up to who he was?" said Sarah.

"By then I guess it was too late," said Jack, turning to Sarah. "He was in the system. Easier to stay as Otto Brendl."

"That is true," said Jayne. "But also with the internet, more and more he felt that those terrible people – they were going to catch up with him. Revenge never goes away for them."

"So that's why he had such security at his cottage?" said Sarah.

"It was partly for his beautiful puppets," said Jayne. "But also he worried the Securitate were getting close. In fact he told me that – just the night before he died – he thought someone had tried to break in."

"While he was in the house?" said Jack.

"Yes. He said nothing was stolen. But he feared the worst."

"Jayne – did he ever tell you his real name?" said Sarah.

"No," said Jayne. "I think perhaps to protect me. But I didn't mind. He was Otto. He'll always be Otto."

Sarah sat back and looked at Jack. His face was stern; was he as moved as she had been by Jayne's story?

"I've told you Otto's secret. What will you do with it?" said Jayne.

"I really don't know," said Jack. "All we were doing was a little background check for the school. Now with this – I have no idea."

"Can't you get his puppets back at least?" said Jayne.

"We still don't know who stole them," said Sarah. "But I guess we

66

can still try – what do you think, Jack?"

"Sure," he said. "But what do we tell Mrs Harper? About Otto?"

Sarah didn't know the answer.

"All that I've told you, it happened a long time ago in a country far away – isn't that the saying?" said Jayne. "Maybe it should just stay that way. I don't think there's anything in the life of Otto Brendl the German jeweller that should concern Mrs Harper."

SARAH WALKED WITH Jack back up the High Street to where he had parked in the village square.

Pretty busy for a weekday he thought, but then remembered – it was the school holidays and the tourist season was in full swing.

He climbed into the little open-top sports car. Sarah leaned against the bonnet.

"So," she said. "Where do we go from here?"

"I don't know," he said. "We're kinda done, aren't we? We found out Otto's secret. Seems to me the only question is what we tell Mrs Harper."

He could see something was troubling her.

"But are we done? What about the missing puppets? Don't you think we should try and get those back – for Otto? For Jayne?"

"Maybe – but the police are already on the case. And they have far more resources than we do."

"Okay. But Jack – come on. Don't you think there's other weird things about this? That guy we saw on the road. The Russian chap asking about you down at the boat yard. Well Russian – Romanian – how would they know the difference? You could be in danger."

"Why?"

Sarah pulled back.

"Something we saw in the cottage maybe? Something else that

Jayne didn't tell us?"

Jack also looked around.

"Or maybe it's just some guy who wants to buy a boat? We haven't seen him since. I can check if he's been down by the river again. Maybe it's not even the same guy."

But Sarah didn't let it go.

"He asked about *you*, Jack. Why?"

Jack nodded, then a small smile. "You must think I have all the answers." Then: "Look, I'll be careful. Remember, I'm kind of used to dealing with bad guys."

Sarah shook her head. "As the target?"

Touché, he thought.

"Okay, I'll be *very* careful. And I will take care of myself. Gotta give Riley a nice long walk. Touch base tomorrow?"

"Great. Daniel's got a match. So, I don't know… If you think we're finished with Otto then maybe I'll go watch. Pretty quiet in the office."

Jack had to wonder if Sarah struggled to make ends meet. She always seemed to have a few web design commissions. But did she get enough of them? She clearly found being an amateur detective a whole lot more fun. Was that why she didn't want this case to be over?

A big SUV drew up next to them. A middle-aged woman with puffy grey hair accompanied by a young woman in summer top, were in the front seats. Mum and daughter out for the day, he guessed.

"Sorry, are you about to go? No parking spaces anywhere!"

Jack looked at Sarah. She shrugged.

"Talk tomorrow, Jack," she said.

"Enjoy the cricket," he said as she turned and headed off to her own car.

Then he smiled at the couple in the car and started the engine.

"All yours."

"Lovely!" the woman said, backing out of the way.

Lovely. And not for the first time he thought, *I'm not in Brooklyn anymore...*

13.

A QUIET NIGHT ON THE GOOSE

RILEY LAY BESIDE Jack, head on his paws. Jack had thought about having a cigar – but on a night like this?

Clear dark sky, no moon yet so the stars were so bright.

Seemed a shame to mess that up with smoke.

Instead, he sat outside on his boat and tried to figure out if Sarah was right about this 'case' not being over.

What had they really learned in the past twenty-four hours?

They now knew that Otto Brendl wasn't German.

That old Otto had in fact come from Romania just before the whole Communist world began to fall apart, just like the Berlin Wall being torn down.

Then – more interesting – that he was in trouble; Brendl was, in fact, in hiding from operatives from the old Romanian secret police.

That – according to Jayne Reid – all these years later – someone still wanted to find him.

Then – do what?

Punish him? Kill him?

But the man just had a heart attack?

Isn't *that* what happened?

At that moment, Riley stood up, stretched. He placed his head near Jack's right hand and Jack gave him a pet.

"Time to head in, Riley?"

The Springer tilted his head left and right.

It was late. But on a night like this, you could just sit out here till dawn.

Might do that sometime, Jack thought.

Worse ways to spend an evening.

The thoughts kept coming…

Someone had tried to break in the night before the puppeteer had died. But according to Jayne, they had failed. Then – only a couple of days later someone had actually gotten in and stolen the puppets.

Krause. Was he lying? Did he have something to do with the stolen, apparently irreplaceable, puppets?

And something else that had been niggling Jack: why hadn't Otto told the police if he was worried about being attacked? Perhaps he feared losing his residency status. But would that outweigh his fear for his life?

And who was the man at Iron Wharf asking after Jack Brennan? In spite of what he'd said to Sarah, he hadn't taken that report lightly.

"More questions here than answers, Riley."

The dog's head bobbed. *Good,* thought Jack. *He agrees.*

For Jack, an imbalance in questions-versus-answers always made him feel uncomfortable.

Riley made a small noise – probably eager for his doggy pillow rather than the wood deck of the ship.

Jack stood up. "Okay, let's head in, boy."

And Riley led the way inside the Grey Goose.

JACK HAD LEFT the wicker case with the Punch and Judy puppets just inside the wheelhouse.

Did those puppets have any value, he thought? They seemed

pretty standard issue as far as puppets went, at least to Jack's untrained eye.

Still – they were all that was left of Brendl's collection.

Now he grabbed the crate by a thick leather handle at one end, and dragged it down the steps and into the galley area. Tomorrow, when it was light, he'd look at them more closely. It was just instinct that had him hold onto them after all of the others had been stolen.

But maybe there was something else there, some 'answer' that he had missed.

Riley found his pillow just inside the bedroom.

"Okay, I'm coming," Jack said.

With the night air, the stars gone, he felt suddenly tired. Despite all his questions, sleep would be good.

Minutes later, the Grey Goose was dark, and the boat completely quiet.

JACK'S EYES OPENED. He had been asleep. He looked at the clock on the small dresser across the room.

2:18. *2:19.*

He usually didn't wake up in the middle of the night. But now —

Riley was standing. The dog walked up to the head of the bed, then did a small circle.

Hearing something. It was probably his paws – the claws on the wooden floor – that had awakened Jack.

Something outside maybe. Bunch of rabbits having a late dinner of greens near the edge of the river. That's all it was…

Jack was about to tell Riley to relax. *Back to sleep. It was nothing.*

He was just about to say the words; the dog was smart and understood a command when he got one.

When Jack heard a noise.

A *rattle*. Hard to place. The sound of something being wiggled, then a creak.

One of the windows near the stern of the boat. Being forced open. They could be latched, but on such a warm night, Jack had left them open.

The sound again, now more measured: someone being careful.

Again Riley did another small circle; he made a noise, not quite a growl, as if he was aware what Jack was thinking.

Better that whoever it is doesn't know we've heard him.

Jack pulled off the sheet, ready to slide out of bed.

Those windows, one on each side, big enough for someone to crawl into the boat.

Another grumble from Riley, louder now, and any chance of surprise would soon evaporate.

It was time for Jack to move.

His bedroom – he still found it hard to call it a cabin – was in the bow of the Grey Goose, separated from the big saloon by a bathroom and walk-in shower.

To get to the far end of the boat he would have to navigate the space in total darkness.

But he'd lived on the Grey Goose for nearly two years now and he knew every inch.

He slid out of the bed and, without making a sound, slipped on a fleece and tracksuit bottoms and found his deck shoes. Then he reached between the bed and the bedside cabinet and slid out the little ASP – the expandable baton he'd brought with him from New York. He swung it in the air and it opened and locked.

Made of carbon steel, light, just thirty inches long – it was a perfect non-lethal weapon to give him an edge if someone attacked. Holding its grip took him back five years to the last time he'd drawn a night-stick in anger.

Like this it had been in the middle of the night – but the setting couldn't have been more different. He'd been with his partner in an alleyway facing down a kid drugged to the eyeballs waving a knife.

But even now, even though he was in a little Cotswold village – there was still the danger of the unknown.

Jack pulled open the door and listened again. Riley was right behind him, seeming to understand the need for total silence.

Another scraping noise from the rear of the boat – and then the unmistakeable sound of footsteps. Jack thought fast. The intruder was coming in through the aft cabin which led directly into the galley.

If he could get there first, he could slip up the stairs to the wheelhouse and have a height advantage over the stranger.

With Riley at his heels, he moved fast through the bathroom and into the saloon, his eyes now adjusting to the darkness. A low moon gave light through the side windows, throwing black shadows across the sofa and the kitchen cabinets.

Another noise from the stern – a door opening – Jack had to be quick.

He found the steps and climbed them as quietly as he could, then ushered Riley behind him into the wheelhouse space and pressed himself into the shadow.

Below, down the steps, he had a good view into the moonlit galley and the saloon but the intruder would have to come right round to this side of the galley to see him.

He realised he was breathing fast.

Cool it, calm down, breathe slow…

The sound of a door opening. Then a shadow. Whoever it was – he was now in the galley, just a few feet away. Jack swallowed – and gripped the baton tightly.

What was the guy doing?

He's waiting. And listening… Jack thought. *But what does he want?*

Then the intruder moved – through the galley and straight to the big wicker case of puppets which lay feet away from the steps. In the darkness Jack could just make out a leather jacket and dark hair. He watched as the figure knelt by the basket and started to undo the buckles on the big leather straps.

It was now or never.

"So what's with the puppets?" he said.

The man spun round incredibly fast and launched himself at Jack who just had time to swing the baton. It caught his attacker on the shoulder with a loud crack but before he could raise his arm again the man had punched Jack hard in the kidneys.

Jack gasped and fell forward, his height and weight pushing his opponent back against the galley worktop. Plates and cups went flying, smashing against the floor. Riley barked.

They hit the ground together and Jack rolled and brought his knee up against the man's groin. His spare hand punched against the side of the man's head. From the wheelhouse Riley leaped at the intruder, tearing at his feet, his teeth bare, snarling. But then the man's hand smashed up into Jack's face and he felt a punch land in his stomach.

Jack felt his baton go flying.

He knew the man was younger, stronger, fitter. And now he had no weapon. The edge was gone.

And he realised with a jolt that he was going to lose this fight – and unless help came it could all go very badly wrong.

He was about to call out, when suddenly the guy broke free and scrambled away up the steps into the wheelhouse. Riley raced after him barking. There was a smash of broken glass and Jack knew the wheelhouse door had been kicked out.

The man had gone.

Riley came back down the wheelhouse steps. Jack lay on the galley floor panting, adrenaline rushing through his veins.

Riley whined and Jack felt him licking at his face. He held the Springer's face between his hands.

75

"Nice work Riley," he said. "We sure had him beat – didn't we?"

He knew that in just a few minutes his whole body would hurt like hell.

But for now he was thankful he was still alive. And aware that he'd been a real fool. He was way too old to be brawling on a kitchen floor…

14.

THE MORNING AFTER

"YOU SHOULD HAVE seen the other guy."

"Not funny, Jack," said Sarah, dabbing his cut eye with cotton wool. "You're too old to be rolling around on the floor fighting."

"Funny you should say that."

Sarah dabbed again and Jack winced. She decided to ignore it. She had come over as soon as Jack had called and told her what had happened, and now she was tending to his wounds as he sat in a deckchair on the top deck of the Grey Goose.

She stretched across the little table and pulled the bowl of antiseptic closer.

"I think Riley and I put up quite a show," he said.

"Some show," Sarah snorted. "From the sound of it, the guy beat you up then left when he was ahead on points."

She saw Riley give her a baleful look from where he lay in his basket in the morning sunshine. Then he looked away, as if embarrassed.

"You were lucky I got here so quickly," she said, carefully sticking a plaster on Jack's cut. "I had a run in with the cricket committee up at the ground. Daniel and I turned up for his game and he was given the third degree because he and his mates had opened up the drinks store in the pavilion on Monday."

"Was that the day he was up there practising?" said Jack. "Doesn't sound like Daniel."

"*Exactly*," said Sarah. "Apparently some booze went missing and the committee didn't know who to blame. Eventually they saw the light and let the kids off. Anyway – he's going to be batting soon so I'll need to get back up there. Don't want to miss his star turn."

"Of course," said Jack. "You can't get these years back."

"Now – lean forwards," said Sarah, inspecting the top of Jack's head where blood was still matted. "I guess you'll live. But I wish you'd taken me more seriously when I warned you yesterday."

"Aw come on Sarah," said Jack, getting up from his deckchair. "Short of staying up all night, that guy was going to get in."

Sarah shrugged, then gathered the used bandages and ointments and went below to dispose of them. Though Jack had swept up down below she could still see signs of the fight everywhere. She looked at the big basket of puppets – at least the intruder hadn't taken them.

"So what do you think now, detective?" she called up the steps. "Case still over?"

"No," came Jack's voice. "Case definitely not over."

Sarah knelt down by the basket and undid the buckles, raising the heavy lid and folding it back. From inside the basket, Otto's puppets stared at her. Punch, Judy, the Policeman, the Devil.

Although they grinned, she felt they were accusing her.

She reached in and picked up Judy and Punch, then went back up the steps, through the damaged wheelhouse and out onto the deck.

"Grab a coffee," said Jack, pointing to the big cafetière that stood on the table.

She laid the two puppets down on the table and poured herself a drink, then sat back in one of the deckchairs.

She took a sip and watched Jack.

"So," she said. "Can you figure this out? Because I can't."

"I know," said Jack, putting his coffee down. "We're missing something here – aren't we? Something really major. There's Otto's secret life, his puppets, the break-ins, the guy attacking me."

"You say he went straight for the basket?"

"Yep."

"So he knew what was in it. And he knew you had it. He must have been following you. Maybe this is all about the puppets. The Punch and Judy."

"You thinking – what if there's something valuable inside them?" said Jack.

"Romanian Crown Jewels?" said Sarah, smiling.

She picked up the Judy. Slipping her hand inside the puppet, she pushed her fingers and thumbs deep into the arms and head. She turned Judy's head to look at Jack and waved the little arms.

"Well, that's not the way to do it," she said. "Nothing in this one."

She slipped the Judy off her hand and put it back on the table.

"I've also been thinking about this whole Securitate thing," she said. "What you said yesterday about the KGB. You know their reputation."

"Yeah?"

"Jack – do you think that possibly Otto's death wasn't a heart attack?"

"Whoa. You mean poison? That's quite a leap. I mean, no real evidence. Though there was that frothing at the mouth."

"Yeah, I saw that too," she said. "I'd almost forgotten. That was strange."

"But I'm no forensics expert," said Jack. "Could be a result of congestion, something normal. And also – how would you administer poison to a guy who's sitting in a theatre made for one, surrounded by screaming kids?"

Sarah reached out and picked up Punch. The face grinned at her, somehow all-knowing.

"You know Grace did some research for me?" said Sarah. "She couldn't find anything on the tattoo. But she did say that poisoning – often undetectable – was one of the favourite methods used by the Eastern bloc security services."

Jack didn't answer. She knew him well enough by now to know that this meant he was taking an idea seriously.

She lifted up the Punch and slid her hand inside the blue-and-white striped costume. Just as her fingers reached for the little hole inside the head, Jack suddenly leapt forward —

"No! Sarah!"

"Ow, Jack, that —"

He grabbed her arm tightly – then carefully pulled the puppet from her grasp. "What the —"

"Sorry Sarah," he said, laying the puppet carefully down on the table. "I suddenly had a thought – what you were just saying – about the Securitate."

She watched as he got up quickly and went over to a locker at the side of the wheelhouse. He pulled out a toolbox and brought it over to the table.

"You ever heard about that guy – Bulgarian I think he was – got murdered in London by the KGB using an umbrella?"

"An umbrella? No – I'm sure I would have remembered…"

"Probably before your time," said Jack, taking out a pair of cutters. "Anyway they jabbed him with an adapted umbrella. It stuck a pellet in him – tiny pellet of poison. Ricin, I think it was. Killed him. Set me thinking…"

Sarah looked on as Jack started to cut the costume off the Punch. Chunks of blue, red-and-white fabric fell onto the table.

"What was in Otto's hand when we found him?" he said.

"The Punch – I think."

"Right. That was the last thing he touched before he died. So what if…"

He put down the clippers, grabbed a torch from the toolbox and handed it to her. Then he held up the remnants of the Punch – little more than a head and arms.

"You've got better eyesight than me," he said. "Take a look. Go on."

Sarah pointed the torch deep inside the puppet and peered in. She didn't really know what she was looking for. But when she saw a sliver of shining metal in the wood and plaster on the head – she knew she'd found it.

She looked at Jack and slowly realised.

"Jack. I was just about to put my hand in here."

"You seen something?"

Sarah nodded.

Jack took the head from her, held it up to the light and reached in with a pair of pliers from the toolbox. It only took a second to pull out the little sliver of metal.

She watched as he held it up to the light.

"The murder weapon, if I'm not mistaken," he said. "See the little reservoir – and the point?"

Sarah nodded. Jack continued:

"I guess Otto put his hand in, jabbed his finger on it – the poison was delivered straight into his blood – and then... His heart just failed."

"That could have killed me," said Sarah.

"Yep, could have," said Jack with a grin. "If I hadn't stopped you. Just think yourself lucky the poison wasn't in the Judy, huh?"

Sarah felt queasy at the thought. But Jack's almost jokey attitude towards her escape was contagious, and suddenly she felt light-headed at having cheated death on this beautiful summer's morning.

"Okay. This is starting to fit together," said Jack, clearly feeling much cheerier now he was back in the chase. "The Securitate guy breaks into Otto's house, plants the poison dart. Otto dies. He breaks in again, hoping to remove the evidence. He steals all the puppets he can find, but —"

"We've got the evidence — or rather, Mrs Harper had it,"

"So he keeps watch on the house, spots us arriving and then leaving with the Punch and Judy…"

"So he breaks in here, hoping to remove it —"

"Not expecting the brave owner and his loyal dog to fight to the death to protect it. Or something like that."

"So Jack — don't you think we ought to tell Alan?"

"Yeah," said Jack. "I guess so. If the killer's that desperate to get the evidence back — I reckon he's still somewhere in the neighbourhood. Not a nice thought."

"Do you think you'd recognise him again?"

"Maybe," said Jack. "I'd certainly recognise the smell. I don't think he's washed for days."

"Mrs Harper will have to know," said Sarah. "It's not going to be good for her. Otto's story will come out — and everyone is going to have to deal with a murder taking place in the school grounds."

"Hmm, not good," said Jack. "But we don't have much choice, Sarah. Not with a killer out there, somewhere."

Sarah stood up.

"I'm going up to the cricket ground. Don't want to miss Daniel. You going to be all right?"

"Sure, I'm fine. Right as rain. Listen — maybe keep this to yourself until I call you, huh? Don't want to get people all worked up."

"You're right. In fact — perhaps we should wait until someone's actually tested that bit of metal? We'll look complete idiots if it's just part of the puppet."

Seeing him with a bandage on his head suddenly made Sarah think that maybe Jack shouldn't be on his own.

The danger might be over. Or it might not.

"You ought to come and watch the match," she said as she

stepped off the gangway onto the riverbank.

"You kidding?" Jack said. "I've seen one of those cricket matches. And it's all been explained to me a dozen times. I have no intention of watching another. Life is too short," Then a grin. "Give Daniel my best!"

Sarah headed down the river path, excited at the thought that once again she and Jack had solved a case.

15.

THE TRUTH ABOUT VULTURES

THERE WAS NO reason to delay bringing the police into this, Jack thought. And with Sarah cheering Daniel on, it was something he could do alone.

If he got any heat from Alan because they delayed, well, he'd catch it, and hopefully be able to explain what they had been doing.

Alan was getting to be a friend – and Jack wanted to keep it that way.

So as he walked up the High Street towards the police station, he began mentally organising the steps that led to their discovery, making sure to include all the information about the mystery attacker, Otto's past, the puppet and the pin... and then his phone rang.

Standing in the shadow of the Village Hall clock tower, he dug it out of his back pocket.

"Hello?"

"Jack, Eddie. Look, I got some new information."

Jack backed off the pavement into a small alleyway. No need for people bustling back and forth on the street to hear his half of the conversation.

"Shoot."

"That tattoo – it was the mark of an inner group in the DSS – the

Romanian Security Services."

"The Securitate," said Jack.

"Well these guys – gotta tell you – they were the baddest of the bad," said Eddie. "Totally ruthless; they were the regime's enforcers, completely above the law. The number of people they made disappear, no questions asked, must have been in the thousands."

Wait a second, Jack thought. That didn't compute. Otto was on the run from the Securitate so —

"Eddie, hang on. You're telling me that if my guy here had *that* tattoo, he was —"

"A monster, Jack. The world's a better place with him gone, you can be sure of that."

For a few moments nothing made sense, the whole carefully constructed tale he was about to tell Alan suddenly turned topsy-turvy.

But then, like the detective he used to be, he started rearranging all the elements.

And a new story – what had to be the *true* story – started to take shape.

'Eddie, can you email the information about that?"

"Already did, buddy. Listen. Your guy with the tattoo might be dead, but those Vulture psychos are still out there, all around the world. So be careful."

Careful. Hearing that a lot these days, Jack thought.

"You got it. And Eddie – thanks."

"Not a problem, Jack. Stay safe."

The call ended. And Jack began to think about what to do next, wishing that Sarah was here rather than at the cricket.

Two heads – with all these facts shuffling – would definitely be better than one. But he knew one place that he had to see right now.

Though getting in might not be easy.

THE BELL TO 'Why Knot' jingled as Jack entered, and he saw Jayne Reid unpacking a box of yarn.

She looked up, quickly putting a properly proprietorial smile on her face before that smile faded at seeing who it was.

"Oh, *you*. I thought we were done —"

Jack figured out the exact tactic he'd use with her. He pointed to the bandage on his face.

"See that?"

"Had a tumble, did we?"

"You might say that. Or maybe someone wanted something from me. And what they wanted… seemed to be Otto's Punch and Judy puppets."

Jayne's face registered true shock. Least her role in this story seemed to be holding up.

"You were attacked?"

"Last night. And I'm thinking, maybe by the same people Otto worried about."

"They're *here*?" She turned away, clearly both confused and stunned by that news. And maybe, Jack guessed, a little scared.

"Jayne, I got attacked last night."

"I assume you've told the police. This —"

Jack held up his hand, "Was about to, but I need…"

He always had trouble lying. Maybe because the truth was so important to him. But for whatever reason, it always felt that anyone could see that he *was* lying.

"I need to know as much as I can about Otto, about those who wanted to harm him. And there's one place that might tell me more."

He took a step towards her. Perhaps her being scared was good. Jayne was a battle-axe of a woman. But she seemed shaken now.

"I need to get into his shop. There may be something there that can tell us about these people. Some secret…"

Her eyes clouded over, and Jack knew that he was onto something here.

"I told you," she said, "I don't —"

Jack raised a hand, nodded… a smile. A move that signalled, *between us, we know that is complete bull* —

"Jayne, I'm just thinking that maybe he kept a spare key. That maybe —"

Another pause.

"— you *know* where that key is." He paused, then: "Those people still want something, even with your Otto dead."

He saw Jayne Reid gulp. Then a nod.

"Okay, I mean, I didn't think it was my business to share, but he gave me a set of keys to the jewellery shop. Just for safekeeping. Didn't think…"

"Thanks," Jack hurried to say before she could change her mind. And Jayne nodded again and opened a low drawer behind the counter.

Jack heard the jangle of keys and then she stood up and handed him a ring with three keys.

"Don't know the order – which opens what."

"I'll figure it out."

In her other hand was a piece of paper. "This is the alarm code. Otto said I should have that too."

Jack took the paper on which was written a string of eight numbers.

"Right. And Jayne – thanks."

And Jack walked out, wondering if she suspected that there might be secrets in the shop that maybe 'Otto' didn't want anyone to know…

Even her.

16.

CLOCKS, JEWELS AND SECRETS

JACK MANAGED TO open the door to the jewellers, and once inside a red light began blinking on a keypad beside the door. He took the piece of paper, entered the sequence of numbers, and the red light stopped blinking.

He waited.

No alarm.

It worked.

And he shut the door.

He didn't know what he was looking for. Many of the jewellery display cases, though locked, were empty.

Probably kept the valuable stuff in a safe somewhere, Jack thought.

He walked around the store, and it occurred to him that somehow this place didn't match the story of 'Otto, the Punch and Judy man'.

Or – for that matter, 'Otto the Securitate Vulture'.

But then, if someone was a killer for a police state, they would know how to wear many masks.

Puppeteer. Jeweller. Recluse.

Killer.

Just then, first one, then all the clocks in the shop began chiming the hour, some with metal ballerinas and silvery bears that emerged with the chimes, while other big wall clocks produced low sonorous bongs.

For a moment it felt as if Jack was standing inside a giant clock.

While some of the chimes still rang, he walked behind the back counter. Wooden drawers sat below the display cases. He pulled open first one, then another, none of the drawers locked.

No secrets hidden here.

He wondered what Alan would say if he spotted Jack in the shop. Nothing terribly legal about this, he thought.

He turned around, and saw a door to the back area.

Might be luckier in there. He opened the door and went in, and immediately felt the dry, stale air. The room was small, claustrophobic. A table, a wooden chair, some papers still there where Otto had left them.

Jack picked them up. An electric bill. An invitation from a school to perform at another fête. A cracked coffee cup with pens, pencils, a sabre-like letter opener.

He turned around and saw the safe: three feet by two and not protected by a combination lock but a keyed entry.

He took the key ring and hoped that he had the right one. He tried the last, slid it in, turned it, and the safe opened.

At first, he could only see the trays of necklaces, rings, brooches. All brightly catching the halogen light that went on inside the safe when the door was open.

But then, he saw a bottom tray, seemingly empty.

Nothing catching light there, nothing sparkling.

Jack reached in and slowly slid out the tray...

"SARAH – I IMAGINE you're in the middle of dinner?"

"Jack. Yes, but I was hoping you'd call. Hold on a minute."

He stood near his car, holding what he'd found inside Otto's shop.

As everything started to fall into place.

"Okay, just wanted to get out of earshot of the kids. Have to remember, they loved old Otto and his shows as well."

He told her about the call from Eddie, about the tattoo and the DSS.

There was silence and for a few seconds, Jack thought the line had gone dead.

"Sarah? You still there?"

"I'm here. I'm just trying to get my head around Otto being… I mean… He was our Punch and Judy man."

Jack waited. And then:

"Right. So – Jayne Reid did have the keys to the shop —"

"I could have guessed that."

"And in the store safe, I found something."

"Go on."

"Brendl's German passport, then his Romanian one. Turns out his real name was Rica Popescu."

"That settles that."

"And that's not all. One more thing: found Popescu's DSS identity card, in full Securitate Uniform. Looking mean, and not a puppet in sight."

"Wow. And you —"

"Took them. Yes. This whole thing is starting to twist on itself."

"Sounds like you almost enjoy that, Jack."

"You know, never thought of it that way, but I imagine I do. When whatever this 'story' was before, slowly flips and – there you are – the truth. Ugly as sin sometimes, but undeniable."

"He was in the secret police, in a secret, brutal branch."

"Yup. The truth. And from the badges and medals on his uniform, he had to be high up."

"So, no one from Securitate was coming after him?"

"But someone was after him, someone from his homeland. I'm thinking that —"

Jack stopped. Directly across the High Street, he saw Costco, now open, shoppers drifting in, grabbing milk, maybe a pack of minced beef for a late summer barbecue.

"Sarah. What you were saying about Daniel? About the storeroom at the Cricket Club being robbed?"

"Yes. I knew he had nothing to do with that."

"As did I."

"He and his friends would never dream of doing that. That field is theirs, the practices, the games, the pavilion serving snacks. It's too much a part of their life."

"Right, okay. So – I know I interrupted your dinner..."

"Let me guess. You want to go somewhere?"

"However did you know?"

"The cricket pitch? You have a hunch?"

"Oh, I'd say at this point it's a bit stronger than a hunch. Could use a guide – especially if anyone sees a big Yank prowling around."

"Let me finish dinner, clean up, get the kids sorted. Say... half eight?"

"I'll pick you up."

"Great, and Jack, I'm beginning to think you know me too well. Drop a hint that there's something *there* and well... I'm *there*."

Jack laughed. "Bet you were a detective in another life. Sherlock Holmes?"

"More like your Watson."

"We take turns. See you in a bit."

And Jack stood there, light fading from the sky, watching the Costco, and wondering if the last bit of this play, their own mysterious Punch and Judy show, was about to end.

17.

THE PAVILION

SARAH LOOKED AT Jack as he parked his little sports car near the cricket pitch, the pavilion not far away.

"You think that the mysterious Romanian, the man who planted the needle to kill Brendl —"

"*Popescu.*"

"Yes – that he had something to do with the pavilion break-in?"

"Makes sense, doesn't it? Needed food – broke into Costco. Needed Dutch courage – broke into the store here. Smelled boozed up when he came at me. Guy like that with his accent would stand out in Cherringham." Jack grinned. "Trust me, I know that."

Sarah looked away.

The pitch was dark, a few lights hitting some areas, but most of it a black sea of grass.

And she had to admit... it did make complete sense.

"Maybe the school break-in too," she said. "I suppose he couldn't check into a hotel if he was planning to kill Popescu. Surprised he even asked about you down at the boatyard."

"Yeah. That had to be a risk for him. And I don't know why learning about me was so important."

"We don't have it all, then."

"No. And then there's this —"

Jack pointed at the pavilion sitting in darkness.

"We know he killed. We know he attacked me on the Goose. And we don't know where he is."

Middle of summer... Sarah thought.

Yet sitting here she felt almost icy.

"Let's go," he said.

Jack popped open the car door, and Sarah followed him, making straight for the buildings ahead.

ALL SEEMED QUIET.

"That the place?" Jack whispered, pointing.

"Yes. There are changing rooms and the bar. And the storeroom for all the gear is round the back."

Jack sniffed. "Let's take a look."

And despite walking beside this tall American detective, a guy who certainly knew how to handle himself – and others – Sarah felt her heart racing.

JACK BENT DOWN, digging out his phone.

He fumbled with it and the phone's light came on, and he aimed it at the lock on the door to the storeroom at the back of the pavilion.

"Been jimmied. See the scratches?"

"You think he broke in here?"

"Let's see."

Jack handed Sarah the phone, and then dug out his wallet. He slipped out a credit card which he worked into the space between the lock and frame, the lock simple, easy to pop open.

"Remind me to give you a call next time I forget my keys," said Sarah.

And since she had the light, Sarah went in first as the door creaked open.

The room was full of bags of cricket gear, stumps, and various equipment for the nets. Otherwise, it was deserted.

But shining the light down, Sarah saw what looked like rubbish on the floor.

She moved the light over the pile. Wrappers from Costco sandwiches, plastic bottles of juice, crumpled empty bags of crisps.

"He was here," she said.

Moving the light a bit, she spotted an empty bottle of Stolichnaya.

"Must have hid here while he planned to kill 'Otto'," Sarah said. "Place deserted, no one ever comes here at night. And from here he could slip out to spy on us, ask questions. Course, he needed food. Question is —"

"Where is he now?"

Jack sighed.

Sarah assumed he had actually hoped to find the guy. That would have tied the whole thing together nicely. Instead, all they had was scattered rubbish showing that the killer had once been here.

"Guess we need to look —"

But Sarah crouched down. She pushed at the collection of wrappers, sandwich containers, plastic bottles, seeing nothing.

And then —

A crumpled piece of paper unlike the others, smaller.

She picked it up.

"Find something?" Jack said.

She used her thumb to smooth it, and saw a train ticket.

London to Cherringham.

Dated one day before Rica Popescu stuck his hand in a puppet and died.

Sarah stood up, the chill — her fear — replaced now with excitement.

"Jack. A train ticket. He came from London, stayed here —"

"And he's not here now."

"He must have gone back."

Jack took the ticket from her.

"Or he's *going* back. Sarah, when is the last train to London?"

Sarah looked away. There was a time she used to have the London-Cherringham schedule memorised. But now —

"God, I don't know. Half nine... ten maybe?"

Jack looked at his watch.

"It's quarter past nine now. It's a long shot. But I'll take any shot we can get. Let's get to the station."

Sarah nodded, and together they ran across the field to his car while she wondered... *how much time do we really have?*

And could the killer have left already?

18.

LAST TRAIN TO LONDON

SARAH HELD TIGHT as Jack made the Sprite screech to a stop next to the stairs that led up from the car park to the platform access.

He didn't worry about finding a space; he just stopped the car.

And as if racing for a train themselves, they bolted up the stairs, Jack taking steps two at a time, while Sarah did her best to keep up. The platform for the London train was on the other side.

She didn't hear any train horns, nothing indicating a train was approaching.

Were they already too late? No, the schedule board still had the last train showing.

Then down the stairs, the whole place eerily deserted, a mid-week London train not getting many customers. On the platform only a few of the station lamps were lit, yellow pools of light in the darkness.

"Careful," Jack said, taking the steps like a twenty-year old. Sarah held the rail as she flew down now as fast as she could.

Until they landed at the bottom, the platform empty.

Until —

"There."

Down at the far end, leaning against the dark window of the ticket office, *someone.*

Easily missed.

Sarah turned in the direction where the train would come from. Still nothing.

"That's him," Jack said quietly.

Jack was about to set after him, but Sarah had an idea. She touched his elbow.

"Jack – I have a feeling…" her voice, a whisper. "This guy, scared, alone."

He turned and looked at her. No movement from the figure indicating that he knew they were discussing him.

Chasing him.

"Let me," she said.

Jack paused a second. Then nodded.

And now Sarah took the lead, walking slightly ahead of Jack, down to the other end of the platform, slowly, deliberately, looking for the first sign of a reaction from the person waiting there.

THEN – HE MOVED. Away from the window. Then another step away.

"He's going to run," Jack said quietly.

And it certainly looked that way, as the figure turned, sweatshirt hood up, now looking at the far end of the platform as if for a way out.

The only way to escape would be across the tracks.

Sarah ran and then, as loud as she could, she shouted: "Please wait!"

The figure hesitated, turning to her.

"We just want to understand. We *know* what you did." Then louder: "We know who Rica Popescu was."

Would that be enough to make him stop? After all his hiding, his plans, his apparent murder of the puppeteer?'

Then, while walking briskly, she said: "We know what kind of man he was."

The man didn't move. Instead, he stayed at the end of the platform, and waited.

And for what seemed like an eternity, Sarah, with Jack trailing, closed the distance between them.

UNDER HIS HOOD, the man's eyes darted back and forth, from Sarah to Jack. Young, thin… he probably could still decide to dash and easily outrun them.

"You police?" he said.

"No," said Sarah. "Not police. We just want to talk to you."

Sarah thought that Jack – the interrogator, the guy who actually did such things – would take over now.

But he didn't. With a nod from him, this chat was hers.

"We know the truth about Otto Brendl. Can you tell us why you came here? Why you did what you did?"

Those eyes, dark, haunted.

Then the man cleared his throat.

"My name is Cezar Dumitru. Twenty years ago, that man and his *vultures* arrested my father. I was a boy. My father – he was a writer, a historian, a scholar! And Popescu tortured him as though he was scum… simply because my father loved history, because he told the *truth*."

The young man was shaking.

It's as if it happened yesterday for him, Sarah thought.

She nodded slowly. Understanding.

The young man continued. "They brought his body to the house. I never saw it. But my mother's sobbing told me all I needed to know. And then, after weeks of her cries, her grief, the accusing looks from neighbours… she jumped into the Dâmbovița river one night. No one could stop her. No one could rescue her. I was alone. Popescu had destroyed my family and my life."

"You were the orphan," Jack said.

Part of this story that Popescu stole to create Otto Brendl.

The man nodded.

"I swore I would track down the killers, and kill them. But Rica Popescu had vanished. It took so long to find the trail, to track him here."

Suddenly, in the distance, a light appeared. The train taking a curve, just a mile away.

The last train to London.

"Why did you stay, Cezar?" said Sarah. "Why didn't you run?"

The young man leaned forward and in the yellow light from the platform lamp she could see his face, drawn, tired.

"I couldn't leave the evidence," he said. "The special poison. I needed to know it was over."

"So you stole the puppets from the cottage," said Jack.

"No," said Cezar. "Somebody else took the puppets. But not the one I wanted."

"So you came to my boat."

Cezar shrugged.

"Now," he said, "you will call the police, arrest me, yes? But I don't care. He is dead, that is all."

The train horn sounded briefly. Cezar had been so close to getting away. Just minutes. Now, they had to… what? Call Alan? Have him arrested?

It all seems wrong, thought Sarah.

Which is when Jack took a step closer, holding something in his hand.

"Here, Cezar. The evidence of who Otto Brendl really was. The monster that you eliminated."

The man took the passports, the Securitate ID.

"Do with them what you wish. No one here needs to know."

"No police?" he said, seeming not to believe them.

"Otto Brendl was a harmless puppeteer who had a heart attack."

"You won't arrest me?"

"For delivering justice?"

Jack shook his head. And this all seemed so right to Sarah.

Cezar looked down at the only evidence of the real Otto Brendl, now in his hands.

The train pulled into the station, slowing, the sudden quiet of the three of them now matched to the shrieks of the train's brakes, then loud squeals as it stopped, followed by the quick *whoosh* of doors opening.

"You have a train to catch, Cezar."

The man nodded, looked to each of them, then smiled.

"Thank you."

"Stay safe," Sarah said.

Then the man in the hoodie turned and climbed onto the train.

And she stood there with Jack, waiting, both of them wanting to see it pull away, the killer getting away.

With the secret and story of Otto Brendl over.

Or as Sarah was about to learn, almost over…

19.

A SURPRISE GIFT

MRS HARPER STOOD up as soon as Sarah and Jack entered her office. Sarah could see that she looked worried, the apprehension so clear in her eyes.

"Please," she said. "Sit – if you can find somewhere. Got a year's worth of paperwork to sort before term's over for me I'm afraid!"

They sat down while the woman looked around as if she had forgotten where she placed her chair, her office desktop still a sea of papers searching for land.

"I have to tell you again how much I appreciate you looking into things."

"It was nothing," Jack said. Then quickly, as if he knew the woman's fears. "Good thing is, we found nothing."

A look at Sarah.

"Really?" Mrs Harper said, practically exhaling the word in relief.

"Nothing at all," Sarah added, she and Jack having planned what they would say. "Of course, Mr Brendl wasn't the best record keeper but it seemed he just lived a quiet life."

Now Mrs Harper beamed.

"That is *so* good to hear. Then the school has nothing to fear."

Jack nodded. "There will be no revelations coming from Otto's cottage."

Interesting parsing of words, Sarah noted.

There might be a risk of something popping up about Brendl's real past. But with his documents gone with his killer, probably to be destroyed, and with Cezar certainly not wanting anyone to know, the secret of Rica Popescu would be safe.

And best of all – Mrs Harper could continue running the school in her disorganised but warm and supportive way. And the children would never have to deal with the real nature of the death which had taken place on that warm Saturday end-of-term morning.

Good all around.

"Oh," Jack said, reaching up to his shirt pocket, "We have something for you."

He handed Mrs Harper a cheque.

"What?" Mrs Harper said, looking up. "This… this is immense. What is this?"

"That's from Max Krause, one of…" Jack glanced again at Sarah.

He's so good at pulling this off.

"… Otto's compatriots, if you will. Does puppet shows. I guess he was so struck by Otto's loss, that, well, he just wanted to do something."

Do something.

Especially after Jack confronted him with the fact that he knew Krause had stolen the puppets. And that a police search of FunLand might not be helpful for business. A shot in the dark there – but it had worked.

As he told Krause, the truth would do no one any good, while a big fat cheque from Krause to the school? Well that would do a lot of good.

"I can't believe it," Mrs Harper said.

"And the best part," Sarah added, "is that Mr Krause has offered to do the annual Punch and Judy show, *gratis*."

"A traditional show," Jack said. "Same as the ones you've always had here. Truncheons and all!"

That made Mrs Harper laugh. It had been the last part of Jack's deal with Krause, one the man quickly agreed to.

Far better than going to jail.

"You two," Mrs Harper said, stuck for words. "The school – and I – we owe you a massive debt."

Jack stood up. "I bet it's all the kids who pass through these halls, and their parents, who owe you a debt, Mrs Harper."

Sarah stood up as well. Mrs Harper still held the cheque as if the amazing item might vanish in her hands.

"Well," she said, "See you both, I hope, at the Autumn Fair!"

And then they left the office, and Sarah could not help but feel that they had done something really good just then.

EXCEPT — She stopped when she reached her car.

"You know, Jack, I have a question."

"Shoot."

"You always seemed like a 'by the book' person to me. And this, all of this, well, certainly doesn't seem like it was by the book at all."

Jack smiled. Not offended by the question.

Of course.

"Well, you see, there are a lot of books. And let's say this one had to have a different ending than most."

"Justice was done?"

"The way I see it? Yes. But I will admit… this has been a tough one. It didn't make sense for a long time, and then —"

"It did."

"Exactly. And without any more innocent people being hurt."

She opened her car door.

"You want a lift?"

"I'm fine," he said. "It's a nice day. I'll walk back down to the boat."

She hesitated a minute. She realised that each time they finished one of their cases, it was almost as if she didn't want to let it go.

At least – that's what she thought this slightly lost feeling was.

So…

"Jack, it's bolognese night. Homemade pasta too. Care to join the family?"

Big grin from Jack. "You had me at 'bolognese'. Wouldn't miss it for the world."

"Seven o'clock?"

"Perfect," he said. "And now that Costco is open again, I'll pick up one of their special reds on the way round."

Then she smiled back and watched as he turned and walked away out of the school car park, heading back to the Grey Goose.

Yes, this case is over, Sarah thought. But she knew: there'd be others.

NEXT IN THE SERIES:

CHERRINGHAM
A COSY CRIME SERIES

THE CURSE OF MABBS FARM

Matthew Costello & Neil Richards

Up on the hill above Cherringham sits Mabbs Farm. It's a place with a dark history going back to the 17th century – a time when locals lived in fear of the devil and witches were burnt at the stake.

Legend has it that the farm – and all who live there – are cursed with misfortune. But is it really just a curse when this year's crops fail, the livestock sicken and deadly fires break out? Or is there a hidden reason behind the dangerous events?

Neither Jack nor Sarah believe in the supernatural – and soon they uncover some very human suspects.

ABOUT THE AUTHORS

Matthew Costello (US-based) and **Neil Richards** (UK) have been writing TV scripts together for more than twenty years. The best-selling Cherringham series is their first collaboration as fiction writers: since its first publication as ebooks and audiobooks the series has sold over a million copies.

Matthew is the author of many successful novels, including *Vacation* (2011), *Home* (2014) and *Beneath Still Waters* (1989), which was adapted by Lionsgate as a major motion picture. He has written for The Disney Channel, BBC, SyFy and has also written dozens of bestselling games including the critically acclaimed *The 7th Guest*, *Doom 3*, *Rage* and *Pirates of the Caribbean*.

Neil has worked as a producer and writer in TV and film, creating scripts for BBC, Disney, and Channel 4, and earning numerous Bafta nominations along the way. He's also written script and story for over 20 video games including *The Da Vinci Code* and *Broken Sword*.